WHAT *the* WORLD *is* READING

Excerpts from a Selection of Bestselling
Paperback Titles from Penguin Group (USA)

| PENGUIN | NAL | BERKLEY | RIVERHEAD |
| BOOKS | ACCENT | | BOOKS |

Published by Penguin, Berkley, Riverhead, and NAL Accent, divisions of
Penguin Group (USA) Inc., 375 Hudson Street,
New York, New York 10014, USA
Penguin Group (Canada), 90 Eglinton Avenue East, Suite 700, Toronto,
Ontario M4P 2Y3, Canada (a division of Pearson Penguin Canada Inc.)
Penguin Books Ltd., 80 Strand, London WC2R 0RL, England
Penguin Ireland, 25 St. Stephen's Green, Dublin 2,
Ireland (a division of Penguin Books Ltd.)
Penguin Group (Australia), 250 Camberwell Road, Camberwell, Victoria 3124,
Australia (a division of Pearson Australia Group Pty. Ltd.)
Penguin Books India Pvt. Ltd., 11 Community Centre, Panchsheel Park,
New Delhi - 110 017, India
Penguin Group (NZ), cnr Airborne and Rosedale Roads, Albany,
Auckland 1310, New Zealand (a division of Pearson New Zealand Ltd.)
Penguin Books (South Africa) (Pty.) Ltd., 24 Sturdee Avenue,
Rosebank, Johannesburg 2196, South Africa

Penguin Books Ltd., Registered Offices:
80 Strand, London WC2R 0RL, England

Excerpt from *Angelology*
© Danielle Trussoni, 2010

Excerpt from *The Beach Trees*
© Harley House Books, LLC, 2011

Excerpt from *Girl in Translation*
© Jean Kwok, 2010

Excerpt from *The Help*
© Kathryn Stockett, 2009

Excerpt from *How to Be an American Housewife*
© Margaret Dilloway, 2010

Excerpt from *My Name Is Mary Sutter*
© Robin Oliveira, 2010

Excerpt from *My Name Is Memory*
© Ann Brashares, 2010

Excerpt from *The Postmistress*
© Sarah Blake, 2010

Excerpt from *The Solitude of Prime Numbers*
© Arnoldo Mondadori Editore S.p.A, 2008 | Translation © Shaun Whiteside, 2009

First published by Penguin, Berkley, Riverhead, and NAL Accent,
divisions of Penguin Group (USA) Inc.

First Printing, 2011
10 9 8 7 6 5 4 3 2 1

Copyright 2011

    REGISTERED TRADEMARKS—MARCA REGISTRADA

PENGUIN BOOKS / NAL ACCENT / BERKLEY / RIVERHEAD BOOKS

Printed in the United States of America

PUBLISHER'S NOTE

Angelology, The Beach Trees, Girl in Translation, The Help, How to Be an American Housewife, My Name Is Mary Sutter, My Name Is Memory, The Postmistress, and *The Solitude of Prime Numbers* are works of fiction. Names, characters, places, and incidents either are the product of the author's imagination or are used fictitiously, and any resemblance to actual persons, living or dead, business establishments, events, or locales is entirely coincidental.

The publisher does not have any control over and does not assume any responsibility for author or third-party Web sites or their content.

If you purchased this book without a cover you should be aware that this book is stolen property. It was reported as "unsold and destroyed" to the publisher and neither the author nor the publisher has received any payment for this "stripped book."

The scanning, uploading, and distribution of this book via the Internet or via any other means without the permission of the publisher is illegal and punishable by law. Please purchase only authorized electronic editions, and do not participate in or encourage electronic piracy of copyrighted materials. Your support of the author's rights is appreciated.

WHAT *the* WORLD *is* READING

CONTENTS

from

Angelology

by

Danielle Trussoni

Sister Evangeline was just a girl when her care was entrusted to the Franciscan Sisters of Perpetual Adoration. Now, at twenty-three, she discovers a 1943 correspondence between the convent's late mother superior and the famous philanthropist Abigail Rockefeller that plunges her into a secret history stretching back a millennium: an ancient conflict between the Society of Angelologists and the monstrously beautiful descendants of angels and humans, the Nephilim. Blending biblical lore, the Miltonic fall of the Rebel Angels, the apocryphal Book of Enoch, and the myth of Orpheus, Angelology *is a luminous, riveting tale of ordinary people caught up in a battle that will determine the fate of the world.*

Devil's Throat Cavern, Rhodope Mountains, Bulgaria

The angelologists examined the body. It was intact, without decay, the skin as smooth and as white as parchment. The lifeless aquamarine eyes gazed heavenward. Pale curls fell against a high forehead and sculptural shoulders, forming a halo of golden hair. Even the robes—the cloth woven of a white shimmering metallic material that none of them could identify exactly—remained pristine, as if the creature had died in a hospital room in Paris and not a cavern deep below the earth.

It should not have surprised them to find the angel in that preserved condition. The fingernails, nacreous as the inside of an oyster shell; the long smooth navel-less stomach; the eerie translucency of the skin—everything about the creature was as they knew it would be, even the positioning of the wings was correct. And yet it was too lovely, too vital for something they had studied only in airless libraries, prints of quattrocento paintings spread before them like road maps. All their professional lives they had waited to see it. Although not one of them would have admitted so, they secretly suspected to find a monstrous corpse, all bones and fiber shreds, like something unearthed from an archaeological dig. Instead there was this: a delicate tapering hand, an aquiline nose, pink lips pressed in a frozen kiss. The angelologists hovered above the body, gazing down in anticipation, as if they expected the creature to blink its eyes and wake.

THE FIRST SPHERE

To you this tale refers,
Who seek to lead your mind
Into the upper day,
For he who overcomes should
Turn back his gaze
Toward the Tartarean cave,
Whatever excellence he takes with him
He loses when he looks below.

—Boethius, *The Consolation of Philosophy*

St. Rose Convent, Hudson River Valley, Milton, New York

December 23, 1999, 4:45 A.M.

Evangeline woke before the sun came up, when the fourth floor was silent and dark. Quiet, so as not to wake the sisters who had prayed through the night, she gathered her shoes, stockings, and skirt in her arms and walked barefoot to the communal lavatory. She dressed quickly, half asleep, without looking in the mirror. From a sliver of bathroom window, she surveyed the convent grounds, covered in a predawn haze. A vast snowy courtyard stretched to the water's edge, where a scrim of barren trees limned the Hudson. St. Rose Convent perched precariously close to the river, so close that in daylight there seemed to be two convents—one on land and one wavering lightly upon the water, the first folding out into the next, an illusion broken in summer by barges and in winter by teeth of ice. Evangeline watched the river flow by, a wide strip of black against the pure white snow. Soon morning would gild the water with sunlight.

Bending before the porcelain sink, Evangeline splashed cold water over her face, dispelling the remnants of a dream. She could not recall the dream, only the impression it made upon her—a wash of foreboding that left a pall over her thoughts, a sensation of loneliness and confusion she could not explain. Half asleep, she peeled away her heavy flannel night shift and, feeling the chill of the bathroom, shivered. Standing in her white cotton briefs and cotton undershirt (standard garments ordered in bulk and distributed biyearly to all the sisters at St. Rose), she looked at herself with an appraising, analytic eye—the thin arms and legs, the flat stomach, the tousled brown hair, the golden pendant resting upon her breastbone. The reflection floating on the glass before her was that of a sleepy young woman.

Evangeline shivered again from the cool air and turned to her clothing. She owned five identical knee-length black skirts, seven black turtlenecks for the winter months, seven black short-sleeved cotton button-up shirts for the summer, one black wool sweater, fifteen pairs of white cotton underwear, and innumerable black nylon stockings: nothing more and nothing less than what was necessary. She pulled on a turtleneck and fitted a bandeau over her hair, pressing it firmly against her forehead before clipping on a black veil. She stepped into a pair of nylons and a wool skirt, buttoning, zipping, and straightening the wrinkles in one quick, unconscious gesture. In a matter of seconds, her private self disappeared and she became Sister Evangeline, Franciscan Sister of Perpetual Adoration. With her rosary in hand, the metamorphosis was complete. She placed her nightgown in the bin at the far end of the lavatory and prepared to face the day.

Sister Evangeline had observed the 5:00 A.M. prayer hour each morning for the past half decade, since completing her formation and taking vows at eighteen years of age. She had lived at St. Rose Convent since her twelfth year, however, and knew the convent as intimately as one knows the temperament of a beloved friend. She had her morning route through the compound down to a science. As she rounded each floor, her fingers traced the wooden balustrades, her shoes skimming the landings. The convent was always empty at that hour, blue-shadowed and sepulchral, but after sunrise St. Rose would swarm with life, a beehive of work and devotion, each room glistening with sacred activity and prayer. The silence would soon abate—the staircases, the community rooms, the library, the communal cafeteria, and the dozens of closet-size bedchambers would soon be alive with sisters.

Down three flights of stairs she ran. She could get to the chapel with her eyes closed.

Reaching the first floor, Sister Evangeline walked into the imposing central hallway, the spine of St. Rose Convent. Along the walls hung framed portraits of long-dead abbesses, distinguished sisters, and the various incarnations of the convent building itself. Hundreds of women stared from the frames, reminding every sister who passed by on her way to prayer that she was part of an ancient and noble matriarchy where all women—both the living and the dead—were woven together in a single common mission.

Although she knew she risked being late, Sister Evangeline paused at the center of the hallway. Here, the image of Rose of Viterbo, the saint after whom the convent had been named, hung in a gilt frame, her tiny hands folded in prayer, an evanescent nimbus of light glowing about her head. St. Rose's life had been short. Just after her third birthday, angels began to whisper to her, urging her to speak their message to all who would listen. Rose complied, earning her sainthood as a young woman, when, after preaching the goodness of God and His angels to a heathen village, she was condemned to die a witch. The townspeople bound her to a stake and lit a fire. To the great consternation of the crowd, Rose did not burn but stood in skeins of flame for three hours, conversing with angels as the fire licked her body. Some believed that angels wrapped themselves about the girl, covering her in a clear, protective armor. Eventually she died in the flames, but the miraculous intervention left her body inviolable. St. Rose's incorrupt corpse was paraded through the streets of Viterbo hundreds of years after her death, not the slightest mark of her ordeal evident upon the adolescent body.

Remembering the hour, Sister Evangeline turned from the portrait. She walked to the end of the hallway, where a great wooden portal carved with scenes of the Annunciation separated the convent from the church. On one side of the boundary, Sister Evangeline stood in the simplicity of the convent; on the other rose the majestic church. She heard the sound of her footsteps sharpen as she left carpeting for a pale roseate marble veined with green. The movement across the threshold took just one step, but the difference was immense. The air grew heavy with incense; the light saturated blue from the stained glass. White plaster walls gave way to great sheets of stone. The ceiling soared. The eye adjusted to the golden abundance of Neo-Rococo. As she left the convent, Evangeline's earthly commitments of community and charity fell away and she entered the sphere of the divine: God, Mary, and the angels.

In the beginning years of her time at St. Rose, the number of angelic images in Maria Angelorum Church struck Evangeline as excessive. As a girl she'd found them overwhelming, too ever-present and overwrought. The creatures filled every crook and crevice of the church, leaving little room for much else. Seraphim ringed the central dome; marble archangels held the corners of the altar. The columns were inlaid with golden halos, trumpets, harps, and tiny wings; carved visages of putti stared from the pew ends, hypnotizing and compact as fruit bats. Although she understood that the opulence was meant as an offering to the Lord, a symbol of their devotion, Evangeline secretly preferred the plain functionality of the convent. During her formation she felt critical of the founding sisters, wondering why they had not used such wealth for better purposes. But, like so much else, her objections and preferences had shifted after she took the habit, as if the clothing ceremony itself caused her to melt ever so slightly and take a new, more uniform shape. After five years as a professed sister, the girl she had been had nearly faded away.

Pausing to dip her index finger into a fount of holy water, Sister Evangeline blessed herself (forehead, heart, left shoulder, right shoulder) and stepped through the narrow Romanesque basilica, past the fourteen Stations of the Cross, the straight-backed red oak pews, and the marble columns. As the light was dim at that hour, Evangeline followed the wide central aisle through the nave to the sacristy, where chalices and bells and vestments were locked in cupboards, awaiting Mass. At the far end of the sacristy, she came to a door. Taking a deep breath, Evangeline closed her eyes, as if preparing them for a greater brightness. She placed her hand on the cold brass knob and, heart pounding, pushed.

The Adoration Chapel opened around her, bursting upon her vision. Its walls glittered golden, as if she had stepped into the center of an enameled Fabergé egg. The private chapel of the Franciscan Sisters of Perpetual Adoration had a high central dome and huge stained-glass panels that filled each wall. The central masterpiece of the Adoration Chapel was a set of Bavarian windows hung high above the altar depicting the three angelic spheres: the First Sphere of Seraphim, Cherubim, and Thrones; the Second Sphere of Dominions, Virtues, and Powers; and the Third Sphere of Principalities, Archangels, and Angels. Together the spheres formed the heavenly choir, the collective voice of heaven. Each morning Sister Evangeline would stare at the angels floating in an expanse of glittering glass and try to imagine their native brilliance, the pure radiant light that rose from them like heat.

Sister Evangeline spied Sisters Bernice and Boniface—scheduled for adoration each morning from four to five—kneeling before the altar. Together the sisters ran their fingers over the carved wooden beads of their seven-decade rosaries, as if intent to whisper the very last syllable of prayer with as much mindfulness as they had whispered the first. One could find two sisters in full habit kneeling side by side in the chapel at all times of the day and night, their lips moving in synchronized patterns of prayer, conjoined in purpose before the white marble altar. The object of the sisters' adoration was encased in a golden starburst monstrance placed high upon the altar, a white host suspended in an explosion of gold.

The Franciscan Sisters of Perpetual Adoration had prayed every minute of every hour of every day since Mother Francesca, their founding abbess, had initiated adoration in the early nineteenth century. Nearly two hundred years later, the prayer persisted, forming the longest, most persistent chain of perpetual prayer in the world. For the sisters, time passed with the bending of knees and the soft clicking of rosary beads and the daily journey from the convent to the Adoration Chapel. Hour after hour they arrived at the chapel, crossed themselves, and knelt in humility before the Lord. They prayed by morning light; they prayed by candlelight. They prayed for peace and grace and the end of human suffering. They prayed for Africa and Asia and Europe and the Americas. They prayed for the dead and for the living. They prayed for their fallen, fallen world.

Blessing themselves in tandem, Sisters Bernice and Boniface left the chapel. The black skirts of their habits—long, heavy garments of more traditional cut than Sister Evangeline's post–Vatican II attire—dragged along the polished marble floor as they made way for the next set of sisters to take their place.

Sister Evangeline sank into the foam cushion of a kneeler, the cover of which was still warm from Sister Bernice. Ten seconds later Sister Philomena, her daily prayer partner, joined her. Together they continued a prayer that had begun generations before, a prayer that ran through each sister of their order like a chain of perpetual hope. A golden pendulum clock, small and intricate, its cogs and wheels clicking with soft regularity under a protective glass dome, chimed five times. Relief flooded Evangeline's mind: Everything in heaven and earth was perfectly on schedule. She bowed her head and began to pray. It was exactly five o'clock.

In recent years Evangeline had been assigned to work in the St. Rose library as assistant to her prayer partner, Sister Philomena. It was an unglamorous position to be sure, not at all as high-profile as working in the Mission Office or assisting in Recruitment, and it had none of the rewards of charity work. As if to emphasize the lowly nature of the position, Evangeline's office was located in the most decrepit part of the convent, a drafty section of the first floor down the hall from the library itself, with leaky pipes and Civil War–era windows, a combination that led to dampness, mold, and an abundance of head colds each winter. In fact, Evangeline had been afflicted with a number of respiratory infections in the past months, causing her a shortness of breath that she blamed entirely on drafts.

The saving grace of Evangeline's office was the view. Her worktable abutted a window on the northeast side of the grounds, overlooking the Hudson

River. In the summer her window would perspire, giving the impression that the exterior world was steamy as a rain forest; in the winter the window would frost, and she would half expect a rookery of penguins to waddle into sight. She would chip the thin ice with a letter opener and gaze out as freight trains rolled alongside the river and barges floated upon it. From her desk she could see the thick stone wall that wrapped about the grounds, an impregnable border between the sisters and the outside world. While the wall was a remnant from the nineteenth century, when the nuns kept themselves physically apart from the secular community, it remained a substantial edifice in the FSPA imagination. Five feet high and two feet wide, it formed a stalwart impediment between worlds pure and profane.

Each morning after her five o'clock prayer hour, breakfast, and morning Mass, Evangeline stationed herself at the rickety table under the window of her office. She called the table her desk, although there were no drawers to its credit and nothing approximating the mahogany sheen of the secretary in Sister Philomena's office. Still, it was wide and tidy, with all the usual supplies. Each day she straightened her calendar blotter, arranged her pencils, tucked her hair neatly behind her veil, and got to work.

Perhaps because the majority of the St. Rose mail came in regard to their collection of angelic images—the main index of which was located in the library—all convent correspondence ended up in Evangeline's care. Evangeline collected the mail each morning from the Mission Office on the first floor, filling a black cotton bag with letters and returning to her desk to sort them. It became her duty to file the letters in an orderly system (first by date, then alphabetically by surname) and respond to inquiries on their official St. Rose stationery, a chore she completed at the electric typewriter in Sister Philomena's office, a much warmer space that opened directly upon the library.

The job proved quiet, categorical, and regular, qualities that suited Evangeline. At twenty-three, she was content to believe that her appearance and character were fixed—she had large green eyes, dark hair, pale skin, and a contemplative demeanor. After professing her final vows, she had chosen to dress in plain dark clothing, a uniform she would keep the rest of her life. She wore no adornments at all except for a gold pendant, a tiny lyre that had belonged to her mother. Although the pendant was beautiful, the antique lyre finely wrought gold, for Evangeline its value remained purely emotional. She had inherited it upon her mother's death. Her grandmother, Gabriella Lévi-Franche Valko, had brought the necklace to Evangeline at the funeral. Taking Evangeline to a bénitier, Gabriella had cleaned the pendant with holy water, fastened the necklace around Evangeline's throat. Evangeline saw that an identical lyre glimmered at Gabriella's neck. "Promise me you will wear it at all times, day and night, just as Angela wore it," Gabriella had said. Her grandmother pronounced Evangeline's mother's name with a lilting accent, swallowing the first syllable and emphasizing the second: An-*gel*-a. She preferred her grandmother's pronunciation to all others and, as a girl, had learned to imitate it perfectly. Like Evangeline's parents, Gabriella had become little more than a powerful memory. The pendant, however, felt substantial against her skin, a solid connection to her mother and grandmother.

Evangeline sighed and arranged the day's mail before her. The time had arrived to get down to work. Choosing a letter, she sliced the envelope with the silver blade of her letter opener, tapped the folded paper onto the table, and read it. She knew instantly that this was not the sort of letter she usually opened. It did not begin, as most of the regular convent correspondences did, by complimenting the sisters on their two hundred years of perpetual adoration, or their numerous works of charity, or their dedication to the spirit of world peace. Nor did the letter include a charitable donation or the promise of remembrance in a will. The letter began abruptly with a request:

Dear St. Rose Convent Representative,

In the process of conducting research for a private client, it has come to my attention that Mrs. Abigail Aldrich Rockefeller, matriarch of the Rockefeller family and patron of the arts, may have briefly corresponded with the abbess of St. Rose Convent, Mother Innocenta, in the years 1943–1944, four years before Mrs. Rockefeller's death. I have recently come upon a series of letters from Mother Innocenta that suggests a relationship between the two women. As I can find no references to the acquaintance in any scholarly work about the Rockefeller family, I am writing to inquire if Mother Innocenta's papers were archived. If so, I would like to request that I might be allowed to visit St. Rose Convent to view them. I can assure you that I will be considerate of your time and that my client is willing to cover all expenses. Thank you in advance for your assistance in this matter.

Yours,

V. A. Verlaine

Evangeline read the letter twice and, instead of filing it away in the usual manner, walked directly to Sister Philomena's office, took a leaf of stationery from a stack upon her desk, rolled it onto the barrel of the typewriter, and, with more than the usual vigor, typed:

Dear Mr. Verlaine,

While St. Rose Convent has great respect for historical research endeavors, it is our present policy to refuse access to our archives or our collection of angelic images for private research or publication purposes. Please accept our most sincere apologies.

Many Blessings,

Evangeline Angelina Cacciatore,

FSPA

Evangeline signed her name across the bottom of the missive, stamped the letter with the official FSPA seal, and folded it into an envelope. After typing out the New York City address on an envelope, she affixed a stamp and placed the letter on a stack of outgoing mail balanced at the edge of a polished table, waiting for Evangeline to take it to the post office in New Paltz.

The response might be perceived by some as severe, but Sister Philomena had specifically instructed Evangeline to deny all access to the archives to amateur researchers, the number of which seemed to be growing in recent years with the New Age craze for guardian angels and the like. In fact, Evangeline had denied access to a tour bus of women and men from such a group only six months before. She didn't like to discriminate against visitors, but there was a certain pride the sisters took in their angels, and they did not appreciate the light cast upon their serious mission by amateurs with crystals and tarot decks.

Evangeline looked at the stack of letters with satisfaction. She would post them that very afternoon.

Suddenly something struck her as odd about Mr. Verlaine's request. She pulled the letter from the pocket of her skirt and reread the line stating that Mrs. Rockefeller may have briefly corresponded with the abbess of St. Rose Convent, Mother Innocenta, in the years 1943–1944.

The dates startled Evangeline. Something momentous had occurred at St. Rose in 1944, something so important to FSPA lore that it would have proved impossible to overlook its significance. Evangeline walked through the library, past polished oak tables adorned with small reading lamps to a black metal fireproof door at the far end of the room. Taking a set of keys from her pocket, she unlocked the archives. Was it possible, she wondered as she pushed the door open, that the events of 1944 were in some way related to Mr. Verlaine's request?

Considering the amount of information the archives contained, they were given a miserly allotment of space in the library. Metal shelves lined the narrow room, storage boxes arranged neatly upon them. The system was simple and organized: Newspaper clippings were filed in the boxes on the left side of the room; convent correspondence and personal items such as letters, journals, and artwork of the dead sisters to the right. Each box had been labeled with a year and placed chronologically on a shelf. The founding year of St. Rose Convent, 1809, began the procession, and the present year of 1999 ended it.

Evangeline knew the composition of the newspaper articles well, as Sister Philomena had assigned her the laborious task of encapsulating the delicate newsprint in clear acetate. After so many hours of trimming and taping and filing the clippings in acid-free cardboard boxes, she felt considerable chagrin at her inability to locate them immediately.

Evangeline recalled with precise and vivid detail the event that had occurred at the beginning of 1944: In the winter months, a fire had destroyed much of the upper floors of the convent. Evangeline had encapsulated a yellowed photograph of the convent, its roof eaten away by flames, the snowy courtyard filled with old-fashioned Seagrave fire engines as hundreds of nuns in serge habits—attire not altogether different from that still worn by Sisters Bernice and Boniface—stood watching their home burn.

Evangeline had heard stories of the fire from the Elder Sisters. On that cold February day, hundreds of shivering nuns stood on the snow-covered grounds watching the convent melt away. A group of foolhardy sisters went back inside the convent, climbing the east-wing staircase—the only passageway still free of fire—and threw iron bed frames and desks and as many linens as possible from the fourth-floor windows, trying, no doubt, to salvage their more precious possessions. The sisters' collection of fountain pens, secured in a metal box, was thrown to the courtyard. It cracked upon hitting the frozen ground, sending inkwells flying like grenades. They had shattered upon impact, exploding in great bursts of colored splotches on the grounds, red, black, and blue bruises bleeding into the snow. Soon the courtyard was piled high with debris of twisted bed springs, water-soaked mattresses, broken desks, and smoke-damaged books.

Within minutes of detection, the fire spread through the main wing of the convent, swept through the sewing room, devouring bolts of black muslin and white cotton, then moved on to the embroidery room, where it incinerated the folds of needlework and English lace the sisters had been saving to sell at the Easter Bazaar, and then finally arrived at the art closets filled with rainbows of tissue paper twisted into jonquils, daffodils, and hundreds of multicolored roses. The laundry room, an immense sweatshop inhabited by industrial-size wringers and coal-heated hot irons, was completely engulfed. Jars of bleach exploded, fueling the fire and sending toxic smoke throughout the lower floors. Fifty fresh-laundered serge habits disappeared in an instant of heat. By the time the blaze had burned down to a slow, steamy stream of smoke by late afternoon, St. Rose was a mass of charred wood and sizzling roof tin.

At last Evangeline came upon three boxes marked 1944. Realizing that news of the fire would have spilled over into the middle months of 1944, Evangeline pulled down all three, stacked them together, and carried them out of the archives, bumping the door closed with her hip. She strode back to her cold, dreary office to examine the contents of the boxes.

According to a detailed article clipped from a Poughkeepsie newspaper, the fire had started from an undetermined quadrant of the convent's fourth floor and spread through the entire building. A grainy black-and-white photograph showed the carcass of the convent, beams burned to charcoal. A caption read, *"Milton Convent Ravaged by Morning Blaze."* Reading through the article, Evangeline found that six women, including Mother Innocenta, the abbess who may or may not have been in correspondence with Mrs. Abigail Rockefeller, had died of asphyxiation.

Evangeline took a deep breath, chilled by the image of her beloved home engulfed in flames. She opened another box and paged through a sheaf of encapsulated newspaper clippings. By February 15 the sisters had moved into the basement of the convent, sleeping on cots, bathing and cooking in the kitchen so that they could assist in repairing the living quarters. They continued their regular routine of prayer in the Adoration Chapel, which had been left untouched by the fire, performing their hourly adoration as if nothing had happened. Scanning the article, Evangeline stopped abruptly at a line toward the bottom of the page. To her amazement she read:

Despite the near-total destruction of the convent proper, it is reported that a generous donation from the Rockefeller family will allow the Franciscan Sisters of Perpetual Adoration to repair St. Rose Convent and their Mary of the Angels Church to their original condition.

Evangeline put the articles into their boxes, stacked them one on top of the other, and returned them to their home in the archive. Edging to the back of the room, she found a box marked EPHEMERA 1940–1945. If Mother Innocenta had had contact with anyone as illustrious as Abigail Rockefeller, the letters would have been filed among such papers. Evangeline set the box on the cool linoleum floor and squatted before it. She found all variety of records from the convent—receipts for cloth and soap and candles, a program of the 1941 St. Rose Christmas celebrations, and a number of letters between Mother Innocenta and the head of the diocese regarding the arrival of novices. To her frustration, there was nothing more to be found.

It was possible, Evangeline reasoned as she returned the documents to their correct box, that Innocenta's personal papers had been filed elsewhere. There were any number of boxes in which she might find them— Mission Correspondence or Foreign Charities seemed especially promising. She was about to move on to another box when she spied a pale envelope tucked below a pack of receipts for church supplies. Pulling it out, she saw that it was addressed to Mother Innocenta. The return address had been written in elegant calligraphy: *"Mrs. A. Rockefeller, 10 W. 54th Street, New York, New York."* Evangeline felt the blood rush to her head. Here was proof that Mr. Verlaine had been correct: A connection between Mother Innocenta and Abigail Rockefeller did, in fact, exist.

Evangeline looked carefully at the envelope and then tapped it. A thin paper fell into her hands.

December 14, 1943

Dearest Mother Innocenta,

I send good news of our interests in the Rhodope Mountains, where our efforts are by all accounts a success. Your guidance has helped the progress of the expedition enormously, and I daresay my own contributions have been useful as well. Celestine Clochette will be arriving in New York early February. More news will reach you soon. Until then, I am sincerely yours,

A. A. Rockefeller

Evangeline stared at the paper in her hands. It was beyond her understanding. Why would someone like Abigail Rockefeller write to Mother Innocenta? What did "our interests in the Rhodope Mountains" mean? And why had the Rockefeller family paid for the restoration of St. Rose after the fire? It made no sense at all. The Rockefellers, as far as Evangeline knew, were not Catholic and had no connection to the diocese. Unlike other wealthy Gilded Age families—the Vanderbilts came immediately to mind—they did not own a significant amount of property in the vicinity. Yet there had to be some explanation for such a generous gift.

Evangeline folded Mrs. Rockefeller's letter and put it into her pocket. Walking from the archives into the library, she felt the difference in temperature in an instant—the fire had overheated the room. She removed the letter she had written to Mr. Verlaine from the stack of mail waiting to be posted and carried it to the fireplace. As the flame caught the edge of the envelope, painting a fine black track into the pink cotton bond, an image of the martyred Rose of Viterbo appeared in Evangeline's mind—a flitting figment of a willowy girl withstanding a raging fire—and disappeared as if carried away in a swirl of smoke.

The A train, Eighth Avenue Express, Columbus Circle station, New York City

T he automatic doors slid open, ushering a gust of freezing air through the train. Verlaine zipped his overcoat and stepped onto the platform, where he was met by a blast of Christmas music, a reggae version of "Jingle Bells" performed by two men with dreadlocks. The groove mixed with the heat and motion of hundreds of bodies along the narrow platform. Following the crowd up a set of wide, dirty steps, Verlaine climbed to the snow-blanketed world aboveground, his gold-wire-rimmed eyeglasses fogging opaque in the cold. Into the arms of an ice-laden winter afternoon he rose, a half-blind man feeling his way through the churning chill of the city.

Once his glasses cleared, Verlaine saw the holiday shopping season in full swing—mistletoe hung at the subway entrance, and a less-than-jolly Salvation Army Santa Claus shook a brass bell, a red-enameled donation bucket at his side. Christmas lights scored the streetlamps red and green. As masses of New Yorkers hurried past, scarves and heavy overcoats warming them against the icy wind, Verlaine checked the date on his watch. He saw, to his great surprise, that there were only two days until Christmas.

Each year hordes of tourists descended upon the city at Christmas, and each year Verlaine vowed to stay away from midtown for the entire month of December, hiding out in the cushioned quiet of his Greenwich Village studio. Somehow he had coasted through years of Manhattan Christmases without actually participating in them. His parents, who lived in the Midwest, sent a package of gifts each year, which he usually opened as he spoke with his mother on the phone, but that was as far as his Christmas cheer went. On Christmas Day he would go out for drinks with friends and then, sufficiently tipsy on martinis, catch an action movie. It had become a tradition, one he looked forward to, especially this year. He'd worked so much in the past months that he welcomed the thought of a break.

Verlaine jostled through the crowd, slush clinging to his scuffed vintage wing tips as he progressed along the salt-strewn walkway. Why his client had insisted upon meeting in Central Park and not in a warm, quiet restaurant remained beyond his imagination. If it weren't such an important project—indeed, if it were not his only source of income at the moment—he would have insisted upon mailing in his work and being done with it. But the dossier of research had taken months to prepare, and it was imperative that he explain his findings in just the right manner. Besides, Percival Grigori had dictated that Verlaine follow orders to the letter. If Grigori wanted to meet on the moon, Verlaine would have found a way to get there.

He waited for traffic to clear. The statue at the center of Columbus Circle rose before him, an imposing figure of Christopher Columbus poised atop a pillar of marble, framed by the sinuous, barren trees of Central Park. Verlaine thought it an ugly, overmannered piece of sculpture, gaudy and out of place. As he walked past, he noticed a stone angel carved into the base of the plinth, a marble globe of the world in its fingers. The angel was so lifelike that it appeared as if it would come unmoored from the monument entirely, lift over the bustle of taxis, and rise into the smoky heavens above Central Park.

Ahead, the park was a tangle of leafless trees and snow-covered walkways. Verlaine went past a hot-dog vendor warming his hands over a gust of steam, past nannies pushing baby carriages, past a magazine kiosk. The benches at the edge of the park were empty. Nobody in his right mind would take a walk on such a cold afternoon.

Verlaine glanced at his watch again. He was late, something he wouldn't worry about under normal circumstances—he was often five or ten minutes behind schedule for appointments, attributing his tardiness to his artistic temperament. Today, however, timing mattered. His client would be counting the minutes, if not the seconds. Verlaine straightened his tie, a bright blue 1960s Hermès with a repeating pattern of yellow fleurs-de-lis that he had won on an eBay auction. When he was uncertain about a situation or felt that he might appear ill at ease, he tended to choose the quirkiest clothes in his closet. It was an unconscious response, a bit of self-sabotage that he noticed only after it was too late. First dates and job interviews were particularly bad. He would show up looking as if he'd stepped out of a circus tent, with every article of clothing mismatched and too colorful for the situation at hand. Clearly this meeting had made him jittery: In addition to the vintage tie, he wore a red pin-striped button-up shirt, a white corduroy sport jacket, jeans, and his favorite pair of Snoopy socks, a gift from an ex-girlfriend. He had really outdone himself.

Pulling his overcoat closer, glad that he could hide behind its soft, neutral gray wool, Verlaine took a deep breath of cold air. He clutched the dossier tight, as if the wind might tear it from his fingers, and walked deeper through the whorls of snowflakes into Central Park.

Beyond the rush of Christmas shoppers, obscured in a pocket of icy tranquillity, a ghostly figure waited upon a park bench. Tall, pale, brittle as bone china, Percival Grigori appeared to be little more than an extension of the swirling snow. He lifted a white silk square from the pocket of his overcoat and, in a violent spasm, coughed into it. His vision trembled and blurred with each seizure and then, in an instant of respite, resumed focus. The silk square had been stained with drops of luminous blue blood, vivid as chipped sapphires in snow. There was no more denying it. His situation had grown increasingly serious in the past months. As he tossed the bloodied silk onto the sidewalk, the skin of his back chafed. His discomfort was such that each small movement felt like an instance of torture.

Percival looked at his watch, a solid-gold Patek Philippe. He'd spoken to Verlaine only the previous afternoon to verify the meeting and had been very clear about the time—twelve o'clock sharp. It was now 12:05. Irritated, Percival leaned into the cold park bench, tapping his cane on the frozen sidewalk. He disliked waiting for anyone, let alone a man he was paying so well. Their telephone conversation the day before had been perfunctory, functional, without pleasantries. Percival disliked discussing business matters over the telephone—he could never quite trust such discussions—yet it took some restraint to resist inquiring after the details of Verlaine's findings. Percival and his family had amassed extensive information about dozens of convents and abbeys across the continent over the years, and yet Verlaine claimed he had come across something of interest just up the Hudson.

Upon their first meeting, Percival had assumed Verlaine to be fresh from business school, a climber who dabbled in the art market. Verlaine had rather wild curly black hair, a self-deprecating manner, and a mismatched suit. He struck Percival as artistic in the way that men were at that time of life—everything from his attire to his manners was too youthful, too trendy, as if he had not yet found his place in the world. He certainly was not the sort Percival usually found working for his family. He later learned that, in addition to his specialization in art history, Verlaine was a painter who taught part-time at a university, moonlighted at auction houses, and took consulting work to get by. He clearly thought himself to be something of a bohemian, with a bohemian lack of punctuality. Nevertheless, the young man had shown himself to be skilled at his work.

Finally Percival spotted him hurrying into the park. As he reached the bench, Verlaine extended his hand. "Mr. Grigori," he said, out of breath. "Sorry to be late."

Percival took Verlaine's hand and shook it, coolly. "According to my exceedingly reliable watch, you are seven minutes late. If you expect to continue to work for us, you will be on time in the future." He met Verlaine's eye, but the young man didn't appear chastened in the least. Percival gestured in the direction of the park. "Shall we walk?"

"Why not?" Glancing at Percival's cane, Verlaine added, "Or we could sit here, if you'd like. It might be more comfortable."

Percival stood and followed the snow-dusted sidewalk deeper into Central Park, the metal tip of the cane clicking lightly upon the ice. Not so very long ago, he had been as handsome and strong as Verlaine and wouldn't have noticed the wind and frost and cold of the day. He remembered once, on a winter walk through London during the 1814 freeze, with the Thames solid and the winds arctic, that he had strolled for miles, feeling as warm as if he were indoors. He was a different being then—he had been at the height of his strength and beauty. Now the chill in the air made his body ache. The pain in his joints drove him to push himself forward, despite the cramping in his legs.

"You have something for me," Percival said at last, without looking up.

"As promised," Verlaine replied, pulling an envelope from under his arm and presenting it with a flourish, his black curls falling over his eyes. "The sacred parchments."

Percival paused, uncertain of how to react to Verlaine's humor, and weighed the envelope in the palm of his hand—it was as large and heavy as a dinner plate. "I very much hope you have something that will impress me."

"I think you'll be quite pleased. The report begins with the history of the order I described on the telephone. It includes personal profiles of the residents, the philosophy of the Franciscan order, notes on the FSPA's priceless collection of books and images in their library, and a summary of the mission work they do abroad. I've cataloged my sources and made photocopies of original documents."

Percival opened the envelope and sifted through the pages, glancing absently at them. "This is all rather common information," he said, dismissive. "I fail to see what could have drawn your attention to this place to begin with."

Then something caught his attention. He pulled a bundle of papers from the envelope and paged through them, the wind ruffling the edges as he unfolded a series of drawings of the convent—the rectangular floor plans, the circular turrets, the narrow hallway connecting the convent to the church, the wide entrance corridor.

"Architectural drawings," Verlaine said.

"What variety of architectural drawings?" Percival asked, biting his lip as he flipped through the pages. The first had been stamped with a date: December 28, 1809.

Verlaine said, "From what I can tell, these are the original sketches of St. Rose, stamped and approved by the founding abbess of the convent."

"They cover the convent grounds?" Percival asked, examining the drawings more closely.

"And the interiors as well," Verlaine said.

"You found these where?"

"In a county-courthouse archive upstate. Nobody seemed to know how they ended up there, and they'll probably never notice that they're gone. After a little searching, I found that the plans were transferred to the county building in 1944, after a fire at the convent."

Percival looked down at Verlaine, the faintest hint of challenge in his manner. "And you find these drawings significant?"

"These are not really your run-of-the-mill drawings. Take a look at this." Verlaine directed Percival to a faint sketch of an octagonal structure, the words ADORATION CHAPEL written at the top. "This is particularly fascinating. It was drawn by someone with a great eye for scale and depth. The structure is so precisely rendered, so detailed, that it doesn't fit at all with the other drawings. At first I thought it didn't belong with the set—it's too different in style—but it has been stamped and dated, like the others."

Percival stared at the drawing. The Adoration Chapel had been rendered with enormous care—the altar and entrance had been given particular attention. A series of rings had been drawn within the Adoration Chapel plan, concentric circles that radiated one from the next. At the center of the spheres, like an egg in a nest of protective tissue, was a golden seal. Flipping through the pages of drawings, Percival found that a seal had been placed upon each sheet.

"Tell me," he said, placing his finger upon the seal. "What, do you suppose, is the meaning of this seal?"

"That interested me, too," Verlaine said, reaching into his overcoat and removing an envelope. "So I did a little more research. It is a reproduction of a coin, Thracian in origin, from the fifth century B.C. The original was uncovered by a Japanese-funded archaeological dig in what is now eastern Bulgaria but was once the center of Thrace—something of a cultural haven in fifth-century Europe. The original coin is in Japan, so I have nothing but this reproduction to go by."

Verlaine opened the envelope and presented Percival with an enlarged photocopied image of the coin.

"The seal was put on the architectural drawings over one hundred years *before* the coin was discovered, which makes this seal—and the drawings themselves—rather incredible. From the research I've done, it seems that this image is unique among Thracian coins. While most from that period depict the heads of mythological figures like Hermes, Dionysus, and Poseidon, this coin depicts an instrument: the lyre of Orpheus. There are a number of Thracian coins in the Met. I went to see them myself. They're in the Greek and Roman Galleries, if you're interested. Unfortunately, there is nothing quite like this coin on display. It's one of a kind."

Percival Grigori leaned on the sweat-slicked ivory knob of the cane, attempting to contain his irritation. Snow fell through the sky, fat, wet flakes that drifted through the tree branches and settled upon the sidewalk. Clearly Verlaine did not realize how irrelevant the drawings, or the seal, were to his plans.

"Very well, Mr. Verlaine," Percival said, straightening himself the best he could and fixing Verlaine with a severe gaze. "But surely you have more for me."

"More?" Verlaine asked, perplexed.

"These drawings you've brought are interesting artifacts," Percival said, returning them to Verlaine with a dismissive flourish, "but they are secondary to the job at hand. If you have obtained information connecting Abigail Rockefeller to this particular convent, I expect you have sought access? What progress there?"

"I sent a request to the convent just yesterday," Verlaine said. "I'm waiting for the response."

"Waiting?" Percival said, his voice rising in irritation.

"I need permission to enter the archives," Verlaine said.

The young man displayed only a slight hesitation, a hint of color in his cheeks, the faintest bafflement in his manner, but Percival seized upon this insecurity with furious suspicion. "There will be no waiting. Either you will find the information that is of interest to my family—information that you have been given ample time and resources to discover—or you will not."

"There's nothing more I can do without access to the convent."

"How long will it take to gain access?"

"It isn't going to be easy. I'll need formal permission to get in the front door. If they give me the go-ahead, it could take weeks before I find anything worthwhile. I'm planning to take a trip upstate after the New Year. It's a long process."

Grigori folded the maps and returned them to Verlaine, his hands shaking. Suppressing his annoyance, he removed a cash-filled envelope from the inside pocket of his overcoat.

"What's this?" Verlaine asked, looking at the contents, his astonishment apparent at finding a pack of crisp hundred-dollar bills.

Percival put his hand upon Verlaine's shoulder, feeling a human warmth that he found foreign and alluring. "It is a bit of a drive up," he said, leading Verlaine along the walkway toward Columbus Circle, "but I believe you have time to make it before nightfall. This bonus will compensate for the inconvenience. Once you've had a chance to complete your work and have brought me verification of Abigail Rockefeller's association with this convent, we will continue our discussion."

from

The Beach Trees

by

Karen White

The moving new novel from national bestselling author Karen White.

From the age of twelve, Julie Holt knew what tragedy can do to a family. At that tender age, her sister disappeared—never to be found. It was a loss that slowly eroded the family bonds she once relied on.

As an adult with a prestigious job in the arts, Julie meets a struggling artist who reminds her so much of her sister, she can't help feeling protective. It is a friendship that begins the process of healing for Julie, and leads her to a house on the Gulf Coast, and to stories of family that take her deep into the past.

CHAPTER 1

The little reed, bending to the force of the wind, soon stood
upright again when the storm had passed over. —Aesop

JULIE

September 2010

Death and loss, they plague you. So do memories. Like the Mississippi's in-cessant slap against the levees, they creep up with deceptive sweetness before grabbing your heart and pulling it under. At least, that's what Monica told me. Monica had been the one with the memories of the great muddy river that cradled the Crescent City, and of the sparkling water of the gulf and the bright white house that sat before it.

My own family settled in Massachusetts about one hundred years after the Pilgrims, and my sturdy New England upbringing left me unprepared and a little in awe of Monica, with her strange accent that curled some words and mispronounced others, that was neither Southern or Northern but a strange combination of both. Her stories of her childhood were sea-soned with the dips and waves of her accent, almost making me forget that Monica had abruptly turned her back on these places that existed so vividly in her memories, and never gone back. Like me, Monica was a self-imposed orphan living and working in New York City, both of us trying very hard to pretend that we belonged there.

I leaned forward in the minivan's driver's seat and glanced in the rear-view mirror at Beau, Monica's motherless little boy, and the fear and anxiety that had been dogging me took hold again. In the last two months I had gone from being a workaholic at a reputable auction house, with no other responsibilities except for my monthly rent and utilities, to the broke, unemployed guardian of a five-year-old boy, possessor of a dilapidated minivan, and apparently the owner of a beach house in Biloxi, Mississippi, with the improbable name of River Song. Despite almost a lifetime spent collecting things, I was at a loss to explain my recent acquisitions.

Beau stirred and I found myself hoping that he would remain asleep for at least another hour. Although we'd stopped overnight in Montgomery, Alabama, listening for endless hours to Disney music was more of a strain on my already raw nerves. For nearly twenty hours we'd been traveling south in a van built during the Reagan administration, through towns and scenery that made me think I'd taken a wrong turn and stumbled into a foreign country. After recalling some of the stories Monica had told me about growing up in the South, I realized that I probably had.

"Mama?"

I looked into the rearview mirror and into greenish blue eyes so much like his mother's, offset by remarkably long and dark eyelashes. Monica said the lashes were from all the Tabasco sauce Louisiana mothers put in their baby's bottles to get them used to hot food. The memory made me smile until Beau looked back at me, his eyes repeating his question.

"No, sweetheart. Your mama isn't here. Remember what we talked about? She's in heaven, watching over you like an angel, and she wants me to take care of you now."

His face registered acceptance, and I looked away before he could see what a fraud I really was. I knew less about Monica's Catholic heaven and angels than I did about raising young children. There was something about this whole experience that was like on-the-job training for a career I'd never wanted.

Beau lifted his left thumb to his mouth, a new habit started shortly after his mother died. In his right hand he held Monica's red knit hat that he placed against his cheek, and began to softly scratch a hole into the knit. It had become his constant companion, along with the dozens of Matchbox cars and LEGOs he managed to secret in his pockets, backpack and pillowcase. Although just barely five, he'd seemed to regress to almost three-year-old behavior since his mother's death, and I didn't know the first thing about how to fix it. Letting him keep his mother's hat had simply seemed a necessity.

"Julie?"

My eyes met his again in the rearview mirror.

"I need to go pee-pee."

I glanced over at the portable GPS that I'd purchased secondhand on eBay. We were in a place called D'Iberville, Mississippi, only about thirty minutes from our final destination. I could picture the beach house Monica had described so clearly in my mind: the wide porch, the rocking chairs, the columns that had always made me think of welcoming arms. My foot pressed heavier on the gas pedal. "Can you hold it just a little longer, Beau? We're almost there."

Scrunching his eyebrows together, he nodded and began to scratch his mother's hat in earnest.

Focusing again on the road in front of me, I began noticing the signs for the Biloxi casinos: Beau Rivage, Isle of Capri, Treasure Bay. None of Monica's stories had included mention of the casinos, leaving me to wonder if it was because they'd been built after Monica left, or because they were as alien to the Gulf Coast as their names.

As I took the Biloxi exit off of Interstate 10 and onto Interstate 110, the GPS showed the van on a narrow strip of road and surrounded by water on both sides as we crossed the Back Bay of Biloxi toward the peninsula nestled between the bay and the Mississippi Sound. I felt hot despite the air-conditioning, my heart pumping a little faster as it suddenly occurred to me the enormity of what I was doing. Heading into the unknown with a five-year-old child no longer seemed like the sanctuary I'd at first imagined as I'd sat in the lawyer's office on Lexington Avenue as he'd handed me a set of house keys, and the name and address of a woman with the unusual name of Ray Von Williams. From twelve hundred miles away, it had all seemed so much more promising than the bleakness of my current situation. Death and loss, they plague you. I sighed, finally beginning to understand what Monica had meant.

The September sun skipped and danced over the water as the road rumbled under the minivan's tires, the constant rhythm doing nothing to dissipate my increased heart rate. The chipper voice of the GPS, whom Beau had named Gertie, instructed me to exit onto Beach Boulevard, the Mississippi Sound running parallel to the road.

High-rises and casinos dominated the landscape to the east. Driving west, I passed the hotels and restaurants with empty parking lots, owing, I assumed, to the time of year. A wide apron of sand banded the sound to my left as I continued west, where on the right side of the road empty lots with only stunted trees and steps leading to nowhere sat next door to houses with new roofs and brightly flowered hedges. The garish colors looked defiant against the scrubby grass yards and plywood windows of their neighbors. A tall, white lighthouse sat nestled between the opposing traffic lanes of the highway, leaning slightly inland.

I recalled a photo of Monica, her brother, and assorted cousins gathered in a pyramid in front of the base. A photo that could belong in any family's album—any family's except for my own.

Nervously, I watched the flag on the GPS show that I was nearing my destination on the right, my thoughts confirmed by Gertie's enthusiastic voice. Flipping on my turn signal, I turned blindly into a driveway and stopped. We had arrived.

I blinked through the windshield, trying to comprehend what I was seeing; trying to understand if the bare boards of wall frames were brand-new, or the hollowed-out guts of a house that had once stood on the site, its porch columns like welcoming arms.

Without looking down, I reached inside my purse for the piece of notepaper where I'd written down the address for the house, to make sure I'd plugged the right one into the GPS: 1100 Beach Boulevard.

Trying to quell my panic, I turned around to face Beau with a forced smile. "I need to check on something. Can you watch the van for me for a minute?"

He hesitated for only a second before nodding. Removing his thumb from his mouth, he said, "I still need to go pee-pee."

I patted his jeans-clad knee. "I know. I'll hurry, okay?"

Leaving the van running, I climbed out onto the crushed-shell drive and slammed the door behind me a little too hard. I smelled the water, then: salty and something else, too, that I couldn't quite identify. Something that reminded me of my own desperation.

Sending Beau a reassuring smile, I walked to the spot where the drive met the road, looking for a mailbox, a painted number—anything that might tell me that this wasn't where I was supposed to be. Not that I hadn't had that exact thought about one hundred times since climbing into the van in New York the day before.

There was an empty lot next door, with short cement steps leading up to nothing but air, and a For Sale sign swinging in the barren and sand-swept yard. On the other side of it sat a modest yellow clapboard cottage with new grass and a freshly swept front walk. More important, it had a mailbox at the end of the driveway. Walking quickly, I stuck to the side of the road, squinting until I could read the house number: 1105.

Using my hand to shield my eyes, I counted off the lots to make sure I'd really found number 1100. I stole a glance across the street that ran perpendicular to Beach Boulevard, and noticed the For Sale signs on empty rectangles of land nestled alongside midcentury homes with thinning trees and new porches. An empty lot near the corner had brick pilings sticking out of the sandy soil like grave markers, casting shadows on the landscape.

Staring back across the street to where I'd left the van, I spotted the old oak, the ancient tree of Monica's stories and paintings. There had once been a tire swing hanging from its thick limbs, leafy branches granting shade on hot Mississippi afternoons. It still stood, but its arms were shorn and stunted, the sparse leaves making the tree look like the balding pate of a man too vain to shave his hair all the way off.

I stumbled back to the car, the enormity of my situation colliding with the pent-up grief and the years spent searching for all I'd lost. I was blinded by it, could barely see the door handle, and fumbled three times before I was finally able to open the door and pull myself into the driver's seat. I grasped the steering wheel, oddly relieved to find something solid beneath my hands, wondering—and hoping—that I might pass out and wake up anywhere else but here.

"Julie?" the little voice called out from the backseat. "I don't need to go pee-pee anymore."

I smelled it then, the sickly tart smell of urine as it saturated the small space inside the van. I sat in shocked silence for a long moment, and then I began to laugh, because it was the only thing I could think of to do.

CHAPTER 2

Landfall: The intersection of the surface center of a tropical cyclone with a coastline.
—National Hurricane Center

After using nearly a full box of hand wipes to clean the seat and Beau, and then putting a clean pair of pants on him while apologizing for not taking him to the bathroom when he'd first told me that he needed to go, I had calmed down enough to think. I handed the little boy a juice box and a bag of Goldfish crackers, then scrambled in my purse and found the notepaper again with Ray Von's name and address on it. I wished there were a phone number, too, since showing up at a stranger's front door unannounced with a little boy in tow wasn't something my New England upbringing had prepared me to do.

As I plugged the address into the GPS, I thought again of how very far from home I really was, and how doing what I'd previously considered unthinkable had become an option only because there was no plan B.

I pulled the van back onto the road and drove east as mapped out on the GPS, Gertie's chirpy voice making me grit my teeth. There was a lot of new construction on this side, mostly of what looked like high-end condos mixed in with the large casinos, and I wondered what had happened to all the houses that had once sat here by the water before gambling had become legal and before the storm.

I took a left onto Bellman Street and the area became residential again, with as many houses as vacant lots lining both sides of the road. At Gertie's direction, I found myself in front of a tiny but neat pale pink house, its single front door painted a glowing yellow and covered by a shingled portico held up by wrought-iron posts. A wreath of green, gold, and purple flowers graced the front door, giving the small house a touch of grandeur. Pots of bright blooms I couldn't name spilled over planters and window boxes. It relaxed me somewhat; I figured that anybody who could do such beautiful things with flowers had to be the kind of person who didn't mind strangers asking for help.

I helped Beau out of his seat and spent a few minutes wiping orange cracker crumbs off of his face and shirt before combing his hair. I wet my thumb as I'd seen Monica do a thousand times, and used it to clean green Magic Marker from his chin. I knew better than to ask him to leave the red hat in the van and instead held out my hand for him to take as I led us to the front door.

I stood still for a long moment, feeling the warm September air that seemed saturated with the scent of salt water and damp vegetation. I couldn't find a doorbell, so I gave a brief knock on the yellow wood and waited. A loud meow caught my attention, and I turned my head to see a fat black cat perched on one of the flowerpots, staring at us with calculating green eyes.

"Kitty cat," Beau said around his thumb.

The cat regarded him silently before leaping from his perch, pausing to brush against Beau's legs before darting off to the side of the house.

"You shouldn't let a black cat cross your path."

Beau and I turned at the sound of the clipped voice with perfect diction, spotting an old woman with skin the color of ash standing in the open doorway. From her hunched back and sticklike arms and legs that were more sinew than flesh, she had to be at least ninety years old. I wasn't sure what I'd been expecting, but it certainly hadn't been an old black woman who didn't seem at all surprised to see me.

I placed my arm around Beau's narrow shoulders, feeling protective. "I'm sorry to bother you, but I'm looking for Ray Von Williams."

The old woman didn't seem to hear me. She was looking at Beau so intently that the little boy pressed his face against my leg, covering his cheek with the hat.

The woman's eyes sharpened, but her voice was soft when she spoke. "That boy's a Guidry." She touched Beau on the shoulder and he shrank back.

Even though he was way too tall and heavy, I bent down and scooped him up. "Are you Ray Von?"

The woman looked steadily at me with eyes that reminded me of clear green marbles. "Yes, I am." She squinted, leaning forward. "Are you Julie Holt?"

I started as unexpected relief settled on me: relief at knowing that I wasn't alone in this empty place of leveled lots and real estate signs. Relief at knowing that somebody knew who I was. It didn't even occur to me to wonder or care how the old woman knew my name. "Yes. Yes, I am. And this is Monica's son, Beau."

The woman smiled, white dentures showing between her lips. "I got something for you." Without another word, she turned into the little house, leaving the door open. Not really having any other options, I squeezed Beau against me and followed Ray Von inside.

I closed the door behind us and entered a small living room where a soap opera played on the television and a collection of papier-mâché masks covered the wall next to the large front window. As I followed the older woman to the back of the house, I paused for a moment, not able to name what was missing.

The next room was the kitchen, with a row of gleaming pots and pans hanging from the ceiling, along with bunches of dried herbs, grasses, and flowers. Something bubbled on the stove, the smell reminding me of Sunday afternoons in Monica's apartment. My stomach grumbled, calling to mind that I hadn't eaten since breakfast and that Beau would need more than crackers and juice.

Ray Von was already stacking telephone books in a sturdy wooden chair at the table, her movements swift and strong, belying her years. "You put Miss Monica's boy here, and I'll get you some red beans and rice."

I placed Beau in the chair after reassuring him that I'd stay next to him, then sat down at the table. Everything seemed so surreal, but I felt myself giving into it as I relaxed against the back of my chair, letting slide the weight of responsibilities and uncertainties, and allowed myself to be taken care of, if only for a short while.

Ray Von stood at the stove using a large ladle to pour red beans over beds of rice she'd already heaped on two plates. When she placed them on the table in front of Beau and me, I noticed that Beau's plate was an old plastic one showing faded images of Mickey Mouse and Donald Duck, and I suddenly realized what had been missing from the living room: family photos. I stared at the plate for a long moment, the cartoon characters at odds with the rustic kitchen and the old woman with no family photographs.

Ray Von filled two plastic tumblers with water from a watercooler by the door and placed them by our plates. "Blow on it first, you hear? I'll be right back."

My stomach rumbling loudly now, I leaned over and stirred Beau's quickly and blew on it, trying not to smell too deeply the heavily scented steam that rose from the plate, because it would make me even hungrier than I already was. After testing Beau's to make sure it was okay to eat, I stuck a fork in my own plate and ate quickly, burning my tongue and having to take a gulp of water to cool it off. But it didn't matter. Nothing seemed to matter anymore.

When Ray Von returned, both of us had nearly empty plates. After leaning a brown-paper-wrapped rectangular package about the size of a placemat against a low cabinet, Ray Von retrieved our plates and scooped second helpings onto them before returning them to the table.

Ray Von sat and folded her hands. "Why are you here with her boy but without Miss Monica?"

My last bite of red beans and rice lodged somewhere in the back of my throat. Slowly, I took a drink from my glass, taking my time to form an answer. It hadn't occurred to me that I'd have to tell the story again. I glanced over at Beau, who had finished eating and was drifting to sleep in his chair, his finger working a hole into the red hat.

I took a deep breath, letting the air fill the space where grief and loss had taken up residence so long ago, then let it out again. "Monica died almost three months ago."

Something flickered in Ray Von's eyes but she didn't look away. Finally, she said, "I suspect it was her heart."

I looked at her in surprise. "How did you know that?"

Her face remained impassive but her bottom lip trembled. "She was dying from the moment she was born. I suppose we all are, but some of us are scheduled from the start."

"I don't understand."

"She was always delicate that way. They called it 'congenital heart disease,' and it's not the first time that family's seen it."

I sat back in my chair, my breath coming so fast that I felt light-headed again. "So she knew she had a weak heart? And didn't do anything?"

"Oh, I don't know if she knew, but I did. I was there when she was born, and I could see it even though the doctors couldn't. Her mama had her tested, too, to be sure, and those doctors still couldn't see anything."

Ray Von stood and took their dirty plates to the sink before she continued. "Some, they can tell when they're born. But others, they don't find out until they're older, and then the heart is so damaged that they need a new one. I'm thinking Miss Monica didn't get her new one in time."

I thought of the last year of Monica's life, of how weak and frail she'd become, of the wait for a new heart. Of how she'd gone to sleep one afternoon and never woke up. But Monica had known long before that, I could see now. She had known and not told me until she couldn't hide it anymore.

Glancing at the wrapped package, I was struck by a thought. "How did you know my name?"

A thin eyebrow went up. "Miss Monica sent it to me with a note. She said the package was for Julie Holt and asked me to hold on to it until you could come and pick it up."

Laughter shouted at us from the television in the other room. "When did she send it?"

Ray Von turned to face me, her back against the sink, her head bobbing in her effort to hold it up high despite her hunched shoulders. "This past February. I hadn't heard one word from that girl for ten years, and then this package arrives with a note that I'm not to open it, and that Julie Holt might come by sometime to pick it up."

I slid my chair back. "Can I see what it is?"

Without answering, Ray Von moved to Beau's chair, where his head had fallen back in sleep, his mouth slightly open. Gently, she smoothed the hair from his forehead. "I loved his granddaddy like he was my own, and then his mama and her brother, too. Hardheaded people, but I loved them. Especially Miss Monica, who was more hardheaded than the rest. She had a sense of right and wrong that would have put a saint to shame. She didn't give a second chance to anybody who didn't live up to her high moral standards." She picked up my glass and moved to the watercooler to refill it. "Especially to those she loved the most."

She kept her back to me for a moment, as if trying to decide whether to tell me anything more, then turned around and placed the tumbler on the table before sitting.

I closed my eyes, trying to corral all the questions that were flitting through my mind, too many to count. "Monica told me stories about her family. About you. They were all happy stories, good memories. They helped me forget. . . ." I shook my head, not wanting to veer down the old path. "But she never told me why she left and never came back. Or why she broke off contact from everyone."

Ray Von was silent for a moment, and I waited, hoping for an answer that would at least explain why I'd driven so far to find something that no longer existed. Instead, Ray Von said, "She used to paint. At first it was just the Guidrys' house here, and the beach and the lighthouse. And then she started painting people—anybody who'd sit still long enough for her. Don't know what happened to all those paintings."

I swallowed, remembering all the landscapes and portraits Monica had painted from memory, like illustrations for her stories. "I think she was on the verge of breaking out. She was scheduled for a big show at a major gallery in New York when she got sick. They had to cancel it." I took a sip of water, needing to wash down the loss that clung to the back of my throat. "We both loved art. That's how we met, actually, at an exhibit of early twentieth-century American portraitists. My great-grandfather, Abe Holt, was one of the featured artists, and he was one of Monica's favorites." Smiling at the memory, I continued. "I was on an awful blind date, and she came up and spilled her drink on him." A small laugh burbled in my throat. "She reminded me so much of my little sister, so petite that her clothes hung on her. I sort of adopted her right then, because she looked like somebody needed to take care of her."

"And the boy? Where is his daddy?"

I paused. "Monica didn't know. The relationship was . . . temporary. He wasn't a part of her life." I clasped my hands tightly in front of me but managed to meet Ray Von's eyes. "Why did she leave? She convinced me to drive all the way down here just from the stories she told me about this place. About her family. But she never told me why she left them."

Ray Von looked away, her eyes shadowed again. "I can't tell you that, because I don't know."

I stared at the older woman, not sure whether I believed her. Finally, I nodded, realizing I wouldn't get another answer. I felt close to tears again, having traveled so many miles, yet arriving no closer to my destination than when I'd left.

"Monica left me her house here, in Biloxi, and guardianship of Beau. I'm not really sure why, because I know she has family. And the house . . ." I stopped, not wanting to revisit it even in my mind. "I guess Hurricane Kat—"

Ray Von held her finger to her lips and shook her head. "We don't say her name out loud around here. Not ever."

I nodded. Even five years later, the hurricane's reminders were everywhere. "I thought that I could just move in with Beau, find a job, and live happily ever after." I pressed my hand over my mouth. The exhaustion of the last months pushed at my head and heart, my isolation suddenly intolerable. Monica had gone to confession every week, and for the first time I could understand why.

I looked up, recalling the Ray Von of Monica's stories, the Ray Von who listened without judgment, and I could no longer hold back the need to unburden myself. "I've never done anything so unplanned or reckless in my life. And I've got this little boy to think of now, and I've brought him here to where we don't even have a bed to sleep in. How could I be so irresponsible?" I bit my lip, wishing now I'd said nothing.

Ray Von leaned toward me, her accent thickening as her diction dropped. "You ain't dead yet, so you ain't done." She stood and retrieved the brown-paper-wrapped package, struggling slightly from the weight of it. I somehow knew that Ray Von would resist any assistance and remained seated. "Don't you go opening it here, now. Miss Monica didn't want me to see it, and I don't want to stir up spirits." She indicated Beau, whose eyes were now open but bleary as he looked around the kitchen as if wondering how he'd gotten there. I almost laughed, thinking that I must have the same look.

The old woman placed the package in front of me. "You got family around here?"

I shook my head, unable to find brief words that would explain my family or why I'd been so eager to adopt Monica—a girl as lost as I was.

"Then you need to take this boy to New Orleans to see his great-grandma Aimee. She'll know what to do."

My finger plucked at the edges of the packing tape, and I recognized the delicate handwriting on the front of the package. "But there had to be a reason why Monica didn't tell them about Beau. What if she didn't want me to take him there? She sent me here, to Biloxi, not New Orleans."

Ray Von leaned closer, her eyes darkening. "Are you going to take that boy and go sleep on an empty lot? Monica's boy needs more than that. You take him home first, then figure out what to do after."

I sat still, listening to dim voices from the television in the other room, and knew I had run out of choices. "I don't have an address."

Her white teeth showed as Ray Von straightened. "Fifteen Twenty First Street. In the Garden District. The pink Victorian with the beautiful garden with the statue."

I took a deep breath, then stood. "Thank you. For the food. For this." I indicated the package. "For the advice. Monica always spoke fondly of you, so I figure you wouldn't tell me wrong."

Ray Von didn't smile. "She left me behind just like she did everybody else. I'm thinking about that boy. He doesn't deserve to be cut off from his family."

I frowned. "Will it be okay with them that, well, that . . ." I wasn't sure how to continue.

"That he doesn't have a daddy? There's some who might care, but not Miss Aimee. She'll love him like he was a prince just because Miss Monica was his mama."

I lifted Beau from the chair, my back feeling the strain. "I'm glad to hear that." Ray Von leaned over to pick up the package, but I stopped her. "Please don't. You've done enough for me already. Let me go put Beau in the car and I'll be right back to get it."

It looked at first as if the old woman would refuse, but then she jutted out her chin instead and nodded. When I returned, Ray Von was in the living room watching another soap opera, the absence of any type of photos or family memorabilia oddly unsettling. I walked past her toward the kitchen to retrieve the package, feeling the solid wood of a frame beneath the paper. I hesitated for a moment inside the doorway. "Thanks again, Ray Von. I appreciate all of your help."

Ray Von didn't raise her gaze from the television, where a blond woman with heavy lip gloss was starting to cry.

"One last thing," I said. She didn't lift her head. "I was wondering if you had the deed to the Biloxi house. If Monica might have sent it to you with the package. She only gave the lawyer the keys."

"I gave you everything I had." She lifted a remote control and raised the volume. "You can close the door behind you on your way out."

Knowing there was nothing else to say, I juggled my load to grab hold of the door handle, then pulled it shut. The black cat that had greeted us on our arrival sat waiting by one of the flowerpots with his tail waving languidly, standing sentry to make sure we left.

Turning my back on the cat, I slid the package into the back of the van, then pulled out of Ray Von's driveway, eager to get away from the odd little house and even odder woman. Remembering the directions to what remained of the beach house, I returned to the street running along the side of it, unable to bring myself to pull into the drive again. Leaving the car running and the air-conditioning on, I slid into the backseat next to Beau and lifted the package onto my lap.

Carefully, I slid a finger under a flap and gently ripped the tape and unfolded the sealed flap at the top. Peering inside, I could make out the top of a thick gilded frame, but nothing else. Placing it on my lap, I continued gently prying off tape and unfolding paper until it was completely unwrapped. I found myself staring at the back of a framed canvas. The whole thing was no more than fifteen inches by eighteen, but it suddenly felt incredibly heavy in my lap. Gingerly, I grasped the edges of the frame and turned it over.

I stared at the portrait, not comprehending exactly what I was looking at, realizing that I'd been expecting to find a painting of the beach house as Monica had remembered it, instead of the ruin it was now. I tamped down my disappointment as I stared instead at the portrait of a beautiful woman with black hair and blue eyes, creamy skin, and a Mona Lisa smile. It showed the woman only from the waist up, but it was clear that she wore some type of ball gown, the material shimmery and midnight blue, an incredible necklace at her long, elegant throat, and earrings of sapphires and diamonds at her ears. Even more remarkable was the stunning brooch of what looked like emeralds and dark green enamel in the shape of an alligator, its tail in an exaggerated point and the eyes glittering red jewels.

It was a striking portrait that seemed to capture the essence of the unknown woman, made her seem alive with active thoughts as her half smile, half smirk regarded me from the canvas. There was something else there, too, something familiar to me that I couldn't quite place. I tried harder, trying to harness the stray thought that wouldn't stop flinging its way through my head like a fish thrown on dry land. And then my gaze came to rest on the artist's signature.

Lifting the frame higher to see it better in the light from the window, I squinted at the florid signature in red paint, not to see it better—my eyesight was perfect—but because I was sure there was some mistake.

"Julie, I'm thirsty."

The voice seemed to come from very far away as I lowered the painting back down to my lap and looked at the little boy sitting next to me, not really seeing him.

Abe Holt. The bright red lines of my great-grandfather's well-known signature danced in my peripheral vision. Abe Holt.

I knew from my experience at the auction house that the painting, assuming it was an authentic Abe Holt, would be worth a considerable amount of money. But why did Monica have it? Monica was always broke; surely she would have sold it at some point. Like when she and Beau were evicted from their apartment for failure to pay their rent. And why would she have left it to me? Monica knew of my family connection to the artist; surely she would have told me about its existence. Unless there was a reason she couldn't.

Slowly, I began to wrap the painting again, even more careful now that I understood its monetary value. Why? The one word continued to reverberate through my head. I slid the painting carefully under the front seat, then gave Beau a juice box.

"I want to go home."

I brushed Beau's dark blond hair from his forehead. "I know, sweetie. Me, too. But we're not done with our adventure yet, okay? But soon."

Not able to stand to see his look of disappointment, I slid up front to the driver's seat and flipped on the GPS. Very carefully, I input the New Orleans address Ray Von had given me. One and a half hours to my destination. After putting the car in drive, I pulled forward onto the road, heading once more to a place foreign to me and away from a past I was beginning to discover didn't want to be left behind.

from

Girl in Translation

by

Jean Kwok

**The "dazzling fiction debut" of heartbreak and love—
and all that gets lost in translation.**
(*Marie Claire*)

When Kimberly Chang and her mother emigrate from Hong Kong to Brooklyn squalor, she begins a secret double life: exceptional schoolgirl during the day, Chinatown sweatshop worker in the evenings. Disguising the more difficult truths of her life—like the staggering degree of her poverty, the weight of her family's future resting on her shoulders, or her secret love for a factory boy who shares none of her talent or ambition—Kimberly learns to constantly translate not just her language but also herself back and forth between the worlds she straddles.

TWO

In that third week of November, I started school. Ma and I had a hard time finding it because it was many blocks away, beyond the area we had explored so far. This new neighborhood was cleaner than the vacant lots and empty storefronts that I had seen closer to our apartment. Aunt Paula had explained with pride that my official address would be different from the one where I actually lived. I should use this other address whenever anyone asked me.

"Why?" I'd asked.

"This is another of Mr. N.'s buildings. It's one you wouldn't be able to afford to live in, but using this address will allow you to go to a better school. Don't you want that?"

"What's the problem with the one I would go to normally?"

"Nothing!" Aunt Paula shook her head, clearly frustrated by my lack of gratitude for what she had done for me. "Go see if your ma needs you."

Now, trying to find this better school, Ma and I walked across several big avenues and then past a number of governmental buildings with statues in front of them. Most of the people on the street were still black, but I saw more whites and lighter shades of black people, possibly Hispanics or other nationalities I couldn't identify yet. I was shivering in my thin jacket. Ma had bought me the warmest one she could find in Hong Kong, but it was still made of acrylic, not wool.

We passed an apartment complex and a park. Finally, we found the school. It was a square concrete building with a large school yard and a flagpole waving the American flag. It was obvious I was late—the yard was empty of people—and we rushed up a broad flight of stairs and pushed open the heavy wooden door.

A black woman in a police uniform sat behind a desk, reading a book. She wore a tag that said "Security."

We showed her the letter from the school. "Go *downda* hall, two *fights up*, classroom's *firsdur left*," she said, pointing. Then she picked up her book again.

I understood only that I had to go that way and so I started slowly down the long hallway. I saw Ma hesitate, unsure whether she was allowed to follow me. She glanced at the security guard, but Ma couldn't say anything in English. I kept going, and at the staircase, I looked back to see Ma in the distance, a thin, uncertain figure, still standing by the guard's desk. I hadn't wished her good luck for her first day at the factory. I hadn't even said good-bye. I wanted to run back and beg her to take me with her, but instead, I turned and made my way up the stairs.

After a bit of searching, I found the classroom and knocked weakly on the door.

A deep, muffled voice came from behind the door. "You're late! Come in."

I pushed it open. The teacher was a man. I learned later his name was Mr. Bogart. He was extremely tall, so that his forehead was level with the top of the blackboard, with a raspberry nose and a head bald as an egg. His green eyes seemed unnaturally light to me in his wide face and his stomach stuck out from under his shirt. He was writing English words on the blackboard, from left to right.

"Our new student *eye-prezoom*?" He gave a strange smile that made his lips disappear, then he looked at his watch and his lips reappeared. "You're very late. What's your *exsu*?"

I knew I had to answer so I guessed. "Kim Chang."

He stared at me for a second. "I know what your name is," he said, enunciating each word. "What's your *exshus*?"

A few of the kids snickered. I took a quick look around: almost all black with two or three white kids. No other Chinese at all, no help in sight.

"Can't you speak English? They said that you did." This came out as a kind of grumbled whine. Who was he talking about? He took a breath. "Why are you late?"

This, I understood. "I sorry, sir," I said. "We not find school."

He frowned, then nodded and waved at an empty desk. "Go sit down. There."

I sat down in the seat he had indicated, next to a chubby white girl with frizzy hair that stuck out in all directions. My fingers were shaking so much that I fumbled with my pencil case. It opened and everything in it clattered on the floor. Now most of the class laughed and I scrambled to pick up my things. I was so flushed I could feel the heat not only in my face but in my neck and chest. The white girl also bent down and picked up a pen and a pencil sharpener for me.

Mr. Bogart continued writing on the blackboard. I sat up straight and folded my hands behind my back to listen even though I couldn't follow it at all.

He glanced at me. "Why are you *see something that*?"

"I sorry, sir," I said, but I had no idea what I'd done wrong this time. I looked around at the other students. Most of them were sprawled in their chairs. Some had sunk so low that they were practically lying down, some were leaning on their elbows, a few were chewing gum. In Hong Kong, students must fold their hands behind their backs when the teacher is talking, to show respect. Slowly, I loosened my arms and placed my hands on the desk in front of me.

Shaking his head, Mr. Bogart turned back to the blackboard.

Our class went to the school cafeteria for lunch. I had never seen children behave the way these Americans did. They seemed to be hanging from the beams on the ceilings, shrieking. The lunchroom ladies roamed from table to table, yelling instructions no one heard. I had followed the other children and slid a tray across a long counter. Different ladies asked me questions and when I only nodded, they plopped foil-covered packages on my plate. I wound up with this: minced meat in the form of a saucer, potatoes that were not round but had been crushed into a pastelike substance, a sauce similar to soy sauce but less dark and salty, a roll and milk. I had hardly ever drunk cow's milk before and it gave me a stomachache. The rest of the food was interesting, although there was no rice, so I felt as if I hadn't really eaten.

After lunch, Mr. Bogart gave out sheets of paper with a drawing of a map.

"This is a pop *quick*," he said. "Fill in *allde captal see T's*."

The other kids groaned but many of them started writing. I looked at my piece of paper and then, in desperation, glanced at the white girl's sheet to try to see what we were supposed to do. Suddenly, the sheet of paper slid out from under my fingers. Mr. Bogart was standing next to me with my test in his hands.

"No *cheap pen*!" he said. His nose and cheeks were flushed as if he were getting a rash. "You a *hero*!"

"I sorry, sir—" I began. I knew he wasn't calling me a hero, like Superman. What had he said? Although I'd had basic English classes in school in Hong Kong, my old teacher's accent did not in any way resemble what I now heard in Brooklyn.

"'I'mmm,'" he said, pressing his lips together. "'I'm sorry.'"

"I'm sorry," I said. My English mistakes clearly annoyed him, although I wasn't sure why.

Mr. Bogart wrote a large "0" on my paper and gave it back to me. I felt as if the zero were fluorescent, blinking in neon to the rest of the class. What would Ma say? I'd never gotten a zero before, and now everyone thought I was a cheat too. My only hope was to impress Mr. Bogart with my industry when we cleaned the classrooms after school. If I'd lost any claim to intelligence here, I could at least show him I was a hard worker.

But when the last bell finally rang, all of the other kids ran out of the room. No one stayed behind to mop and sweep the floors, put up the chairs or clean the blackboards.

Mr. Bogart saw me hesitating and asked, "Can I help you?"

I didn't answer and hurried from the classroom.

Ma was waiting for me outside. I was so happy to see her that when I took her hand, my eyes became hot.

"What is it?" she said, turning my face to her. "Did the other children tease you?"

"No." I wiped my cheeks with the back of my hand. "It's nothing."

Ma looked at me intently. "Did some child hit you?"

"No, Ma," I said. I didn't want to worry her when there was so little she could do. "Everything is different here, that's all."

"I know," she said, still looking concerned. "What did you do today?"

"I don't remember."

Ma sighed, then gave up and started teaching me how to get to the factory by myself. She went through a long list of things for me to be careful of: strange men, homeless people, pickpockets, touching the dirty railing, standing too close to the edge of the platform, etc.

Once we passed the entrance of the subway, the roar of an incoming train blocked out her words. Behind the grimy windows, we could see the walls of the tunnels speed by in a blur. There was so much noise that Ma and I could speak little on the subway ride there. There were two boys about my age sitting across from us. As the taller one got up, a bulky knife fell out of his pocket. It was sheathed in leather, the black handle grooved to fit a large hand. I pretended I wasn't looking and willed myself to be invisible. The other boy gestured, the first one picked it up, and then they left the train. I peeked at Ma and she had her eyes closed. I huddled closer to her and concentrated on learning the stops and transfers so I wouldn't get lost by myself.

When we got out of the train station, Ma turned to me and said, "I wish you didn't have to take the subway by yourself."

That was the first time. Going to the factory after school would become something so automatic that sometimes, even when I needed to go someplace else years later, I would find myself on the trains to the factory by accident, as if that were the place to which all roads led.

....

Chinatown looked very much like Hong Kong, although the streets were less cramped. The fish store was piled high with sea bass and baskets of crabs; grocery store shelves were stocked with canned papayas, lichee nuts and star fruit; peddlers on the street sold fried tofu and rice gruel. I felt like skipping beside Ma as we passed restaurants with soy sauce chickens hanging in the window and jewelry stores that glittered with yellow gold. I could understand everyone without any effort: "No, I want your best winter melons," one woman said; "That's much too expensive," said a man in a puffy jacket.

Ma brought us to a doorway that led to a freight elevator. We took the elevator upstairs and exited. When Ma pushed open the metal door of the factory, the heat rushed out and wrapped itself around me like a fist. The air was thick and tasted of metal. I was deafened by the roar of a hundred Singer sewing machines. Dark heads were bent over each one. No one looked up; they only fed reams of cloth through the machines, racing from piece to piece without pausing to cut off the connecting thread. Almost all the seamstresses had their hair up, although some strands had escaped and were plastered to the sides of their necks and cheeks by the sweat. They wore air filters over their mouths. There was a film of dirty red dust on the filters, the color of meat exposed to air for too long.

The factory took up the entire floor of a massive industrial building on Canal Street. It was a cavernous hall bulging with exposed beams and rusting bolts covered in ever-thickening layers of filth. There were mountains of fabric on the floor next to the workers, enormous carts piled high with half-finished pieces, long metal racks hung with the pressed and finished clothes. Ten-year-old boys rushed across the floor dragging carts and racks from section to section. The fluorescent light swirled down to us through the clouds of fabric dust, bathing the tops of the women's heads in a halo of white light.

"There's Aunt Paula," Ma said. "She was out collecting rent earlier."

Aunt Paula strode across the factory floor with a load of red fabric in her arms, distributing work to the seamstresses. The ones to whom she gave the bigger loads seemed grateful, nodding repeatedly to show their thanks.

Now she had seen us and she came over.

"There you are," she said. "The factory is impressive, isn't it?"

"Older sister, can I talk to you?"

I could see this wasn't the response she wanted. Her face seemed to tighten, and then she said, "Let's go to the office."

Although no one dared to stare openly, the workers' eyes followed us as we walked with Aunt Paula to Uncle Bob's office at the front of the factory. We passed women using machines I had never seen before to hem pants and sew on buttons. Everyone worked at a frantic pace.

Through the window of the office door, we could see Uncle Bob sitting behind a desk. His walking stick leaned against the wall next to him. We entered and Aunt Paula closed the door behind us.

"First day, eh?" Uncle Bob said.

Before we had a chance to reply, Aunt Paula spoke. "I'm sorry, but we don't have much time," she said. "I can't let the other workers think I'm showing you any favoritism, just because you're family."

Ma said, "Of course not. I know you're both very busy and you haven't seen the apartment we're in, but it is not very clean." Ma meant that it was below acceptable living standards. "And I don't believe it is a safe place for *ah*-Kim."

"Oh, little sister, don't worry," Aunt Paula said, with such warmth and reassurance in her voice that I believed her despite myself. "It is only temporary. There was no place else available that you would be able to afford, not with the many expenses you have. But Mr. N. has many buildings, and as soon as another place opens up that you can pay for, we will move you there."

Ma visibly relaxed, and I could feel myself beginning to smile again.

"Now, come," Aunt Paula continued, "we'd better all get back to work before the employees think we're having a family party in here."

"Good luck," Uncle Bob called as we left.

Aunt Paula walked us to our workstation, passing an enormous table I hadn't seen earlier. A combination of very old ladies and young children were crowded around it, clipping all the extraneous threads off the sewn garments. This seemed to be the easiest job.

"They enter at this table as children and they leave from it as grandmas," Aunt Paula said with a wink. "The circle of factory life."

From there, we walked into an enormous cloud of steam. I could hardly see but I realized that this was where most of the heat was coming from. Four massive steaming stations were connected to a central boiler that made a loud hissing sound every few minutes as air escaped from it. One man stood in front of each station, placing garments on the surface of the steamers, then slamming the lid shut, expelling huge gusts of steam. Each man had a large sawhorse where he piled the pressed pieces for "finishing," which was Ma's job. The piles were already growing.

Finally, we reached our work area at the back of the factory. It was larger than our entire apartment. There was a long table and a towering stack of pressed clothing, which we were to hang, sort, belt or sash, tag and then bag in a sheath of plastic. Aunt Paula left us with the warning that the shipment was going out in a few days, and Ma and I were expected to get everything done on time.

....

Ma hurried to start hanging up the pants and she asked me to sort by size an enormous rack filled with pants already on hangers. She gave me an air filter as well, a rectangular piece of white cloth tied behind the ears, but we were next to the steamer section. The heat was stifling. I felt as if I couldn't breathe and took it off after a few minutes. Ma didn't wear hers either.

I spotted a wrinkled piece of Chinese newspaper in the industrial trash can and stealthily took it. It gave me heart to see the familiar characters. I spread it out on an empty stool next to me as I began my sorting.

After less than an hour in the factory, my pores were clotted with fabric dust. A net of red strands spread themselves across my arms so that when I tried to sweep myself clean with my hand, I created rolls of grime that tugged against the fine hairs on my skin. Ma constantly wiped off the table where she was working, but within a few minutes, a layer would descend, thick enough for me to draw stick figures in if I'd had the time. Even the ground was slick with dust, and whenever I walked, the motion displaced rolls of filth that tumbled and floated by my feet, lost.

Something mingled with the stink of polyester in my nostrils. I turned around. A boy was standing next to me. He was about my size, dressed in an old white T-shirt, but there was a tension in his shoulders and arms that told me he was a fighter. His eyebrows were thick, crossing his face in one line, and underneath them, his eyes were a surprising golden brown. He was munching on a roasted pork bun. The crisp crust glistened and I could almost taste the sweet and luscious meat in my mouth.

"You can still read Chinese," he said, cocking his head at the newspaper.

I nodded. I didn't mention that it was all I could read.

"I forgot everything. We've already been in America for five years." He was showing off now. "You must be smart, reading and all." This wasn't a compliment, it was a question.

I decided to be honest. "I used to be."

He thought about this a second. "Eat a bite?"

I hesitated. It isn't Chinese to eat from someone else's food. No kid in Hong Kong had ever offered any to me.

The boy waved the bun under my nose. "Come on," he said. He ripped off a clean piece and held it out.

"Thanks," I said, and popped it in my mouth. It was as delicious as it had smelled.

"You can't tell though." He spoke with his mouth full. "I swiped it from Dog Flea Mama's station."

I stared at him, confused and appalled. "Who?" I'd already swallowed my part of the theft.

"The Sergeant." A sergeant is any cruel person in a position of authority.

I must have still looked confused.

He sighed. "Dog. Flea. Mama. You must have seen her." Then he scratched himself on the neck, a perfect imitation of Aunt Paula's habit.

I gasped. "That's my aunt!"

"Ay yah!" His eyes were wide.

Then I started to laugh and he did too.

"I don't normally take things, you know. I just like bothering her. Come find me at the thread-cutters' when you take a break. My name's Matt," he said.

....

When Ma urged me to take a break later, I edged up to the thread-cutters' counter. The tiny old ladies and kids were busy examining the garments in their hands, snipping off the excess threads with special scissors that spring back open after each cut. Some of the children were as young as five years old. I spotted Matt working with fast hands next to a younger boy in glasses. A woman who must have been their mother sat next to the smaller boy. She wore large rose-tinted glasses that barely covered the enormous bags under her eyes.

When the mother saw me, she squinted through her thick lenses.

"Are you a boy or a girl?" she asked. Matt stifled a laugh.

I knew I looked like a boy, completely flat-chested, with my hair cut short by Ma because of the Hong Kong heat. I wished I could disappear.

The other boy next to Mrs. Wu was slight, with glasses that dangled from his protruding ears. He didn't look up. He only kept working on the same skirt. As I watched, he turned it over again and again, looking for threads he had missed. On the table next to him was a toy motor-cycle with a color picture of an American Indian printed on the gas tank. It looked worn, as if it had been chewed upon.

"Hello," I said to him.

When the boy didn't respond, Matt leaned over and gently waved his hand in front of the boy's face. He made some gestures with his hand that looked like a kind of sign language. The boy looked up and then immediately turned his gaze downward again. In that brief glance, I saw that his eyes seemed unfocused behind the glasses.

"Park doesn't hear so well," Mrs. Wu said.

"Ma, I'm taking a break," Matt said, and he jumped off his stool. He turned to Park and made a few more gestures. I thought probably he was asking if Park wanted to come with us.

When Park didn't react at all, Matt turned to me and said, "He's shy."

"Don't be too long," Mrs. Wu said. "There's a lot of work that needs to be done."

Some of the other kids gravitated to us when they saw that we were free, and we all moved toward the soda machine by the entrance. It cost twenty cents per bottle and I learned later that few people actually purchased from it because of the expense, but the idea of getting a cold soda in the sweltering factory was so attractive that the soda machine was a popular hangout anyway.

I suspected that most of the other kids were at the factory for the same reasons I was. They weren't officially employed by the factory, but there was no place else for them to go, and their parents needed their help. As Ma had explained earlier, all employees were secretly paid by the piece; this meant that the work the children did was essential to the family income. When I was in high school, I learned that piece payment was illegal, but those rules were for white people, not for us.

Leaning against the humming soda machine, I could see Matt was the leader of the factory kids. They seemed to range in age from about four to teens. To save money, Ma made many of my clothes herself, even though she couldn't do it very well, so I had on a home-sewn shirt while the other kids were wearing cool T-shirts with English sayings like "Remember to Vote." They interspersed their Chinese with English to show off how Americanized they were and everyone apparently knew I was fresh off the boat. There was some whispering when they found out Dog Flea Mama was my aunt, but Matt seemed to have taken me under his wing and no one dared tease me. Despite the hard work, I was relieved to be among Chinese kids again.

After ten minutes, though, everyone started wandering back to the work they knew awaited them if they ever wanted to leave. I returned to Ma and resumed work but I was exhausted. I'd been there for three hours. I kept waiting for Ma to say it was time to go home. Instead, she pulled out a container of rice cooked with carrots and a bit of ham: we would have dinner at the finisher's table. I couldn't complain. She'd been there much longer than I had. We ate standing up and as fast as we could so we could get enough work done to stay on schedule. That first night, we left at nine o'clock. Later, I discovered that this was considered early.

The next morning, I stayed in the tiny bathroom a long time.

"Kim," Ma said. "We'll be late for school."

I reluctantly opened the door, clutching my thin towel. "I don't feel well."

She looked concerned and placed her hand on my forehead. "What is it?"

"I have a stomachache," I said. "I think I should stay home today."

Ma studied me, then smiled. "Silly girl, why are you talking the big words?" She was asking why I was lying. "You have to go to school." Ma believed in the absolute sanctity of education.

"I can't," I said. My eyes started tearing up again, even though I tried to hide it by rubbing my face with the towel.

"Are the other children mean to you?" she asked kindly.

"It's not the kids," I said. I stared at the splintered threshold of the bathroom. "It's the teacher."

Now she looked skeptical. Teachers are highly respected in Hong Kong. "What are you talking about?"

I told her the whole story, the way Mr. Bogart had corrected my accent yesterday, the way he'd been angry at the things I hadn't understood, that he'd thought I'd been cheating and given me a zero. I couldn't stop them now, I let the tears brim over but kept myself from breaking into full sobs.

When I was finished, Ma was silent. She had to work her mouth a moment before she was able to speak. Then she said haltingly, "Maybe I could talk to him and tell him what a good student you are."

For a moment, my heart caught flight but then I pictured Ma talking to Mr. Bogart with the few English words she knew. It would only make him despise me more. "No, Ma, I will try harder."

"I am sure that if you work the way you always do, he will give you another chance." She reached out and pulled me to her. She laid her cheek against the top of my head.

I was surprised and grateful Ma hadn't automatically taken the teacher's side against me. Leaning against her, I closed my eyes and pretended for just a moment that everything would be all right.

After my talk with Ma about Mr. Bogart, I did what any sensible kid would: I started playing hooky. Ma had no choice but to leave me to walk to school alone because she had to get to the factory as early as possible in order to have any hope of finishing our work on time. She couldn't afford the luxury of escorting me again.

"Are you sure you know the way?" Ma asked. "Do you have your token for the subway after school?"

Ma was afraid to leave me alone but now that I'd done it before, the route to school was actually simple. The distance was long but it required few turns. We arrived at her subway station first. Ma hesitated at the entrance, but I nodded as confidently as I could, then headed off in the direction of the school. As soon as she was out of sight, I ducked around the corner and circled home.

Despite the cold, I was sweating. What if I ran into Mr. Bogart or one of the kids from my class recognized me? I'd never done anything similar before. Like any good Chinese girl, I'd always followed the rules and been glad to be praised by the teachers. But the only alternative was going into Mr. Bogart's classroom again. I was learning about desperation.

It was with a sick feeling that I pulled open the heavy door to our building and entered into that dark mouth. I huddled in the dirty living room, still in my jacket, with the weak sun's rays clogged in the murky windows. I hadn't ever really been alone before. I felt a bit safer sitting in the center of the mattress where I could at least see any roaches coming before they got to me. Anything could materialize in the emptiness beyond the shadowy doorway. When the garbage bags covering the windows in the kitchen rustled, I thought about how easy it would be for a burglar to rip off the tape and step inside. I would jump out of the window on the street side if someone broke in. If I hung from the windowsill by my fingers before dropping, I would probably live. That became my solution for all the contingencies that flashed across my mind: if the stove caught on fire, if a ghost appeared in the bathroom, if a rat attacked, if Ma walked through the door looking for something she'd forgotten.

The apartment air felt damp and raw. It was November of what would turn out to be one of the most bitter winters in New York's history. To keep myself from becoming too chilled and scared, I flicked on the small television. Its busy chatter brought me into the world of dishes and lemon-scented sprays. There were a lot of shows about hospitals: doctors kissing nurses, nurses kissing patients; there were films about cowboys and Indians; shows with people sitting in squares with flashing lights. In particular, the commercials mystified me: "Raise your arms to be sure," the voice boomed, showing men and women thrusting their arms into the air. Why should you do this? Was it something to do with the Liberty Goddess?

"Triple your vocabulary in thirty days," the authoritative male voice promised. "*Impess* your friends. Show your boss who's boss." I sat up straighter. I imagined myself going back to class, using words even Mr. Bogart didn't know. Then came a commercial for alphabet soup, the concept of which fascinated me, as all things in letter form did. I realized it was almost lunchtime and I was hungry.

I braved the darkened kitchen to peek into the small refrigerator. Ma wasn't used to having one and it was mostly empty. I found only a few small pieces of leftover chicken, the bones protruding from under the fatty skin, some yellowing vegetables with cold rice, and a shallow container of oyster sauce. I didn't dare touch anything. I'd been taught that everything had to be thoroughly heated. The kids in a commercial I'd just seen were eating cheese sandwiches with apples and milk, but there was no bread here, let alone anything to put on it. I was afraid even to get a glass of water by myself; back home, I'd gotten such bad diarrhea from drinking unboiled tap water that I'd almost died. Ma had always made a warm snack for me when we came home from school together: steamed mackerel in black beans, roasted pork skins, winter melon soup, fried rice with scallions.

My stomach rumbled as I continued to watch TV. Gleaming toy kitchens, bouncing balls large enough for kids to sit on, kids eating cookies in tree houses. There was a commercial with a family at a long table laden with food. I longed for the room in the background of that table. It was so clean there you could have lain down on the floor. In our apartment, I didn't dare to touch much. Even after our rigorous cleaning, everything seemed shrouded with the dust of dead insects and mice. I indulged in one of my favorite fantasies, that Pa had stayed alive. If he were here, maybe we wouldn't have had to work at the factory at all. Maybe he'd have been able to get a regular job and help us build up a life like those people on TV.

Even with the television, the day stretched out long and gray through the empty hours, and I kept thinking about Ma working alone at the factory. I could see her neat hands moving slowly over the pressed clothes. I imagined how tired she must be but I couldn't go to join her yet because I had to pretend to be at school. I jumped when a mouse ran across the floorboards and disappeared into the kitchen. I kept the broom by me, for both intruders and roaches, and when roaches started scurrying across the wall by the mattress, I made noise with the broom to keep them at a distance, careful not to squash them. This was partly due to my Buddhist training to care for all life, but it was mostly because I didn't want to see them smeared across the wall.

Out of boredom, I started looking through Ma's things. In her suitcase, I found a square piece of cardboard carefully bound with twine. I could tell it was an old 78 rpm record, the kind that played only one song per side. It must have held great emotional value for her. There was no other reason for her to keep it; we didn't even have a record player here. I opened the case carefully, expecting something from a Chinese opera, and was surprised to find an Italian one instead. I read the label: it was Caruso singing Cavaradossi's aria "E lucevan le stelle," from *Tosca*. A photograph fluttered to the floor. Then I remembered:

Our apartment in Hong Kong, the ceiling fan humming as I lay on the sofa, Ma playing a record for me before bedtime. That had been our nightly routine, one song and then bed. Usually she chose Chinese music, but this one night she had put on a man singing with sorrow in another language, the words escaping him in gasps of regret. She had turned away then. When I could see her face again, she had composed herself and showed me no more of her feelings.

I had gone to bed that night, and many nights since, thinking about Ma's life and the grief that connected her to that music. I knew her parents had been landowners and intellectuals, and for that, they'd been unfairly sentenced to death during the Cultural Revolution. Before they died, they had spent all the wealth they had left to get Ma and Aunt Paula out of China and into Hong Kong before it was too late. And then Ma's true love, my pa, had been taken from her far too young, only in his early forties, going to bed with a headache one evening to die of a massive stroke later that night.

I picked up the photograph that had fallen from the record album. It was the one Ma had framed and kept on the piano in our living room in Hong Kong. Like many people in Hong Kong then, we didn't have a camera because it was too expensive, and so this was the only photo I'd seen of the three of us. Despite the stiffness of the pose, the three heads were slightly inclined toward one another, like a true family. Ma looked lovely, with her small neat features and pale skin stretched tight over her bones, and Pa was the perfect accompaniment: dark luminous eyes, handsome and sculpted, like a movie star. I looked at the size of his hands, one of which was tenderly—it seemed to me—cupping the child's elbow, my elbow. That was a heroic hand, a hand that would take over a heavy plow, a hand to save you from demons and muggers. And me, balanced on Pa's knee, about two years old, and peering curiously at the camera. I was wearing a sailor's outfit and my hand was raised to my forehead in a military salute, no doubt the photographer's idea. Lucky child: had I really been so cute, had I ever been so happy?

A few characters had been scrawled on the back. Our names and the date. I knew it wasn't Ma's handwriting, so it had to be his. I ran my finger over the impressions the pen had made in the thick paper. This was my pa, his hand had written these words.

This was all I had to take the place of memory. However, no matter how great my loss, Ma's was even greater. She had actually known and loved him, and his death had left her alone to raise and support me. I carefully put the record and the photograph back. I wanted more than ever to be by Ma's side, helping her in any way I could.

Finally, I could leave for the factory. I passed by a street cart with a sign that said "Hot Dogs." The vendor was selling thin sausages in rolls with yellow sauce on top. It looked and smelled delicious, but I had only a subway token and a dime for emergency phone calls in my pocket. On the subway, I felt as if everyone was staring at me: that kid didn't go to school today. I saw other kids with backpacks going into the train station and I hoped I wouldn't see anyone who recognized me. A policeman stood by the token booth, a gun slung from his belt, and he stared at me as I put my token in the slot.

"Hey!" he said.

I froze, ready to be arrested. But he was looking at another kid who had thrown a crumpled paper bag on the floor.

"You pick that up!" he said.

I passed through and ran down to the train platform.

from

The Help

by

Kathryn Stockett

Aibileen is a black maid in 1962 Jackson, Mississippi, raising her seventeenth white child. She's always taken orders quietly, but lately it leaves her with a bitterness she can no longer bite back. Her friend Minny has certainly never held her tongue, or held on to a job for very long, but now she's working for a newcomer with secrets that leave her speechless. And white socialite Skeeter has just returned from college with ambition and a degree but, to her mother's lament, no husband. Normally Skeeter would find solace in Constantine, the beloved maid who raised her, but Constantine has inexplicably disappeared.

Together, these seemingly different women join to work on a project that could forever alter their destinies and the life of a small town—to write, in secret, a tell-all book about what it's really like to work as a black maid in the white homes of the South. Despite the terrible risks they will have to take, and the sometimes humorous boundaries they will have to cross, these three women unite with one intention: hope for a better day.

AIBILEEN

CHAPTER 1

August 1962

MAE MOBLEY was born on a early Sunday morning in August 1960. A church baby we like to call it. Taking care a white babies, that's what I do, along with all the cooking and the cleaning. I done raised seventeen kids in my lifetime. I know how to get them babies to sleep, stop crying, and go in the toilet bowl before they mamas even get out a bed in the morning.

But I ain't never seen a baby yell like Mae Mobley Leefolt. First day I walk in the door, there she be, red-hot and hollering with the colic, fighting that bottle like it's a rotten turnip. Miss Leefolt, she look terrified a her own child. "What am I doing wrong? Why can't I stop it?"

It? That was my first hint: something is wrong with this situation.

So I took that pink, screaming baby in my arms. Bounced her on my hip to get the gas moving and it didn't take two minutes fore Baby Girl stopped her crying, got to smiling up at me like she do. But Miss Leefolt, she don't pick up her own baby for the rest a the day. I seen plenty a womens get the baby blues after they done birthing. I reckon I thought that's what it was.

Here's something about Miss Leefolt: she not just frowning all the time, she skinny. Her legs is so spindly, she look like she done growed em last week. Twenty-three years old and she lanky as a fourteen-year-old boy. Even her hair is thin, brown, see-through. She try to tease it up, but it only make it look thinner. Her face be the same shape as that red devil on the redhot candy box, pointy chin and all. Fact, her whole body be so full a sharp knobs and corners, it's no wonder she can't soothe that baby. Babies like fat. Like to bury they face up in you armpit and go to sleep. They like big fat legs too. That I know.

By the time she a year old, Mae Mobley following me around everwhere I go. Five o'clock would come round and she'd be hanging on my Dr. Scholl shoe, dragging over the floor, crying like I weren't never coming back. Miss Leefolt, she'd narrow up her eyes at me like I done something wrong, unhitch that crying baby off my foot. I reckon that's the risk you run, letting somebody else raise you chilluns.

Mae Mobley two years old now. She got big brown eyes and honey-color curls. But the bald spot in the back of her hair kind a throw things off. She get the same wrinkle between her eyebrows when she worried, like her mama. They kind a favor except Mae Mobley so fat. She ain't gone be no beauty queen. I think it bother Miss Leefolt, but Mae Mobley my special baby.

I LOST MY OWN BOY, Treelore, right before I started waiting on Miss Leefolt. He was twenty-four years old. The best part of a person's life. It just wasn't enough time living in this world.

He had him a little apartment over on Foley Street. Seeing a real nice girl name Frances and I spec they was gone get married, but he was slow bout things like that. Not cause he looking for something better, just cause he the thinking kind. Wore big glasses and reading all the time. He even start writing his own book, bout being a colored man living and working in Mississippi. Law, that made me proud. But one night he working late at the Scanlon-Taylor mill, lugging two-by-fours to the truck, splinters slicing all the way through the glove. He too small for that kind a work, too skinny, but he needed the job. He was tired. It was raining. He slip off the loading dock, fell down on the drive. Tractor trailer didn't see him and crushed his lungs fore he could move. By the time I found out, he was dead.

That was the day my whole world went black. Air look black, sun look black. I laid up in bed and stared at the black walls a my house. Minny came ever day to make sure I was still breathing, feed me food to keep me living. Took three months fore I even look out the window, see if the world still there. I was surprise to see the world didn't stop just cause my boy did.

Five months after the funeral, I lifted myself up out a bed. I put on my white uniform and put my little gold cross back around my neck and I went to wait on Miss Leefolt cause she just have her baby girl. But it weren't too long before I seen something in me had changed. A bitter seed was planted inside a me. And I just didn't feel so accepting anymore.

"GET THE HOUSE straightened up and then go on and fix some of that chicken salad now," say Miss Leefolt.

It's bridge club day. Every fourth Wednesday a the month. A course I already got everthing ready to go—made the chicken salad this morning, ironed the tablecloths yesterday. Miss Leefolt seen me at it too. She ain't but twenty-three years old and she like hearing herself tell me what to do.

She already got the blue dress on I ironed this morning, the one with *sixty-five* pleats on the waist, so tiny I got to squint through my glasses to iron. I don't hate much in life, but me and that dress is *not* on good terms.

"And you make sure Mae Mobley's not coming in on us, now. I tell you, I am so burned up at her—tore up my good stationery into five thousand pieces and I've got fifteen thank-you notes for the Junior League to do..."

I arrange the-this and the-that for her lady friends. Set out the good crystal, put the silver service out. Miss Leefolt don't put up no dinky card table like the other ladies do. We set at the dining room table. Put a cloth on top to cover the big L-shaped crack, move that red flower centerpiece to the sideboard to hide where the wood all scratched. Miss Leefolt, she like it fancy when she do a luncheon. Maybe she trying to make up for her house being small. They ain't rich folk, that I know. Rich folk don't try so hard.

I'm used to working for young couples, but I spec this is the smallest house I ever worked in. It's just the one story. Her and Mister Leefolt's room in the back be a fair size, but Baby Girl's room be tiny. The dining room and the regular living room kind a join up. Only two bathrooms, which is a relief cause I worked in houses where they was five or six. Take a whole day just to clean toilets. Miss Leefolt don't pay but ninety-five cents an hour, less than I been paid in years. But after Treelore died, I took what I could. Landlord wasn't gone wait much longer. And even though it's small, Miss Leefolt done the house up nice as she can. She pretty good with the sewing machine. Anything she can't buy new of, she just get her some blue material and sew it a cover.

The doorbell ring and I open it up.

"Hey, Aibileen," Miss Skeeter say, cause she the kind that speak to the help. "How you?"

"Hey, Miss Skeeter. I'm alright. Law, it's hot out there."

Miss Skeeter real tall and skinny. Her hair be yellow and cut short above her shoulders cause she get the frizz year round. She twenty-three or so, same as Miss Leefolt and the rest of em. She set her pocketbook on the chair, kind a itch around in her clothes a second. She wearing a white lace blouse buttoned up like a nun, flat shoes so I reckon she don't look any taller. Her blue skirt gaps open in the waist. Miss Skeeter always look like somebody else told her what to wear.

I hear Miss Hilly and her mama, Miss Walter, pull up the driveway and toot the horn. Miss Hilly don't live but ten feet away, but she always drive over. I let her in and she go right past me and I figure it's a good time to get Mae Mobley up from her nap.

Soon as I walk in her nursery, Mae Mobley smile at me, reach out her fat little arms.

"You already up, Baby Girl? Why you didn't holler for me?"

She laugh, dance a little happy jig waiting on me to get her out. I give her a good hug. I reckon she don't get too many good hugs like this after I go home. Ever so often, I come to work and find her bawling in her crib, Miss Leefolt busy on the sewing machine rolling her eyes like it's a stray cat stuck in the screen door. See, Miss Leefolt, she dress up nice ever day. Always got her makeup on, got a carport, double-door Frigidaire with the built-in icebox. You see her in the Jitney 14 grocery, you never think she go and leave her baby crying in her crib like that. But the help always know.

Today is a good day though. That girl just grins.

I say, "Aibileen."

She say, "Aib-ee."

I say, "Love."

She say, "Love."

I say, "Mae Mobley."

She say, "Aib-ee." And then she laugh and laugh. She so tickled she talking and I got to say, it's about time. Treelore didn't say nothing till he two either. By the time he in third grade, though, he get to talking better than the President a the United States, coming home using words like *conjugation* and *parliamentary*. He get in junior high and we play this game where I give him a real simple word and he got to come up with a fancy one like it. I say *house cat*, he say *domesticized feline*, I say *mixer* and he say *motorized rotunda*. One day I say *Crisco*. He scratch his head. He just can't believe I done won the game with something simple as *Crisco*. Came to be a secret joke with us, meaning something you can't dress up no matter how you try. We start calling his daddy *Crisco* cause you can't fancy up a man done run off on his family. Plus he the greasiest no-count you ever known.

I tote Mae Mobley into the kitchen and put her in her high chair, thinking about two chores I need to finish today fore Miss Leefolt have a fit: separate the napkins that started to fray and straighten up the silver service in the cabinet. Law, I'm on have to do it while the ladies is here, I guess.

I take the tray a devil eggs out to the dining room. Miss Leefolt setting at the head and to her left be Miss Hilly Holbrook and Miss Hilly's mama, Miss Walter, who Miss Hilly don't treat with no respect. And then on Miss Leefolt's right be Miss Skeeter.

I make the egg rounds, starting with ole Miss Walter first cause she the elder. It's warm in here, but she got a thick brown sweater drooped around her shoulders. She scoop a egg up and near bout drop it cause she getting the palsy. Then I move over to Miss Hilly and she smile and take two. Miss Hilly got a round face and dark brown hair in the beehive. Her skin be olive color, with freckles and moles. She wear a lot a red plaid. And she getting heavy in the bottom. Today, since it's so hot, she wearing a red sleeveless dress with no waist to it. She one a those grown ladies that still dress like a little girl with big bows and matching hats and such. She ain't my favorite.

I move over to Miss Skeeter, but she wrinkle her nose up at me and say, "No, thanks," cause she don't eat no eggs. I tell Miss

Leefolt ever time she have the bridge club and she make me do them eggs anyways. She scared Miss Hilly be disappointed.

Finally, I do Miss Leefolt. She the hostess so she got to pick up her eggs last. And soon as I'm done, Miss Hilly say, "Don't mind if I do," and snatch herself two more eggs, which don't surprise me.

"Guess who I ran into at the beauty parlor?" Miss Hilly say to the ladies.

"Who's that?" ask Miss Leefolt.

"Celia Foote. And do you know what she asked me? If she could help with the Benefit this year."

"Good," Miss Skeeter say. "We need it."

"Not that bad, we don't. I told her, I said, 'Celia, you have to be a League member or a sustainer to participate.' What does she think the Jackson League is? Open rush?"

"Aren't we taking nonmembers this year? Since the Benefit's gotten so big?" Miss Skeeter ask.

"Well, yes," Miss Hilly say. "But I wasn't about to tell *her* that."

"I can't believe Johnny married a girl so tacky like she is," Miss Leefolt say and Miss Hilly nod. She start dealing out the bridge cards.

I spoon out the congealed salad and the ham sandwiches, can't help but listen to the chatter. Only three things them ladies talk about: they kids, they clothes, and they friends. I hear the word *Kennedy*, I know they ain't discussing no politic. They talking about what Miss Jackie done wore on the tee-vee.

When I get around to Miss Walter, she don't take but one little old half a sandwich for herself.

"Mama," Miss Hilly yell at Miss Walter, "take another sandwich. You are skinny as a telephone pole." Miss Hilly look over at the rest a the table. "I keep telling her, if that Minny can't cook she needs to just go on and fire her."

My ears perk up at this. They talking bout the help. I'm best friends with Minny.

"Minny cooks fine," say ole Miss Walter. "I'm just not so hungry like I used to be."

Minny near bout the best cook in Hinds County, maybe even all a Mississippi. The Junior League Benefit come around ever fall and they be wanting her to make ten caramel cakes to auction off. She ought a be the most sought-after help in the state. Problem is, Minny got a mouth on her. She always talking back. One day it be the white manager a the Jitney Jungle grocery, next day it be her husband, and ever day it's gone be the white lady she waiting on. The only reason she waiting on Miss Walter so long is Miss Walter be deaf as a doe-nob.

"I think you're malnutritioned, Mama," holler Miss Hilly. "That Minny isn't feeding you so that she can steal every last heirloom I have left." Miss Hilly huff out a her chair. "I'm going to the powder room. Y'all watch her in case she collapses dead of hunger."

When Miss Hilly gone, Miss Walter say real low, "I bet you'd love that." Everbody act like they didn't hear. I better call Minny tonight, tell her what Miss Hilly said.

In the kitchen, Baby Girl's up in her high chair, got purple juice all over her face. Soon as I walk in, she smile. She don't make no fuss being in here by herself, but I hate to leave her too long. I know she stare at that door real quiet till I come back.

I pat her little soft head and go back out to pour the ice tea. Miss Hilly's back in her chair looking all bowed up about something else now.

"Oh Hilly, I wish you'd use the guest bathroom," say Miss Leefolt, rearranging her cards. "Aibileen doesn't clean in the back until after lunch."

Hilly raise her chin up. Then she give one a her "ah-hem"s.

She got this way a clearing her throat real delicate-like that get everbody's attention without they even knowing she made em do it.

"But the guest bathroom's where the help goes," Miss Hilly say.

Nobody says anything for a second. Then Miss Walter nod, like she explaining it all. "She's upset cause the Nigra uses the inside bathroom and so do we."

Law, not this mess again. They all look over at me straightening the silver drawer in the sideboard and I know it's time for me to leave. But before I can get the last spoon in there, Miss Leefolt give me the look, say, "Go get some more tea, Aibileen."

I go like she tell me to, even though they cups is full to the rim.

I stand around the kitchen a minute but I ain't got nothing left to do in there. I need to be in the dining room so I can finish my silver straightening. And I still got the napkin cabinet to sort through today but it's in the hall, right outside where they setting. I don't want a stay late just cause Miss Leefolt playing cards.

I wait a few minutes, wipe a counter. Give Baby Girl more ham and she gobble it up. Finally, I slip out to the hall, pray nobody see me.

All four of em got a cigarette in one hand, they cards in the other. "Elizabeth, if you had the choice," I hear Miss Hilly say, "wouldn't you rather them take their business outside?"

Real quiet, I open the napkin drawer, more concerned about Miss Leefolt seeing me than what they saying. This talk ain't news to me. Everwhere in town they got a colored bathroom, and most the houses do too. But I look over and Miss Skeeter's watching me and I freeze, thinking I'm about to get in trouble.

"I bid one heart," Miss Walter say.

"I don't know," Miss Leefolt say, frowning at her cards. "With Raleigh starting his own business and tax season not for six months...things are real tight for us right now."

Miss Hilly talk slow, like she spreading icing on a cake. "You just tell Raleigh every penny he spends on that bathroom he'll get back when y'all sell this house." She nod like she agreeing with herself. "All these houses they're building without maid's quarters? It's just plain dangerous. Everybody knows they carry different kinds of diseases than we do. I double."

I pick up a stack a napkins. I don't know why, but all a sudden I want a hear what Miss Leefolt gone say to this. She my boss. I guess everbody wonder what they boss think a them.

"It would be nice," Miss Leefolt say, taking a little puff a her cigarette, "not having her use the one in the house. I bid three spades."

"That's exactly why I've designed the Home Help Sanitation Initiative," Miss Hilly say. "As a disease-preventative measure."

I'm surprised by how tight my throat get. It's a shame I learned to keep down a long time ago.

Miss Skeeter look real confused. "The Home...the what?"

"A bill that requires every white home to have a separate bathroom for the colored help. I've even notified the surgeon general of Mississippi to see if he'll endorse the idea. I pass."

Miss Skeeter, she frowning at Miss Hilly. She set her cards down faceup and say real matter-a-fact, "Maybe we ought to just build you a bathroom outside, Hilly."

And Law, do that room get quiet.

Miss Hilly say, "I don't think you ought to be joking around about the colored situation. Not if you want to stay on as editor of the League, Skeeter Phelan."

Miss Skeeter kind a laugh, but I can tell she don't think it's funny. "What, you'd...kick me out? For disagreeing with you?"

Miss Hilly raise a eyebrow. "I will do whatever I have to do to protect our town. Your lead, Mama."

I go in the kitchen and don't come out again till I hear the door close after Miss Hilly's behind.

WHEN I KNOW MISS HILLY GONE, I put Mae Mobley in her playpen, drag the garbage bin out to the street cause the truck's coming by today. At the top a the driveway, Miss Hilly and her crazy mama near bout back over me in they car, then yell out all friendly how sorry they is. I walk in the house, glad I ain't got two new broken legs.

When I go in the kitchen, Miss Skeeter's in there. She leaning against the counter, got a serious look on her face, even more serious than usual. "Hey, Miss Skeeter. I get you something?"

She glance out at the drive where Miss Leefolt's talking to Miss Hilly through her car window. "No, I'm just...waiting."

I dry a tray with a towel. When I sneak a look over, she's still got her worried eyes on that window. She don't look like other ladies, being she so tall. She got real high cheekbones. Blue eyes that turn down, giving her a shy way about her. It's quiet, except for the little radio on the counter, playing the gospel station. I wish she'd go on out a here.

"Is that Preacher Green's sermon you're playing on the radio?" she ask.

"Yes ma'am, it is."

Miss Skeeter kind a smile. "That reminds me so much of my maid growing up."

"Oh I knew Constantine," I say.

Miss Skeeter move her eyes from the window to me. "She raised me, did you know that?"

I nod, wishing I hadn't said nothing. I know too much about that situation.

"I've been trying to get an address for her family in Chicago," she say, "but nobody can tell me anything."

"I don't have it either, ma'am."

Miss Skeeter move her eyes back to the window, on Miss Hilly's Buick. She shake her head, just a little. "Aibileen, that talk in there... Hilly's talk, I mean..."

I pick up a coffee cup, start drying it real good with my cloth.

"Do you ever wish you could... change things?" she asks.

And I can't help myself. I look at her head-on. Cause that's one a the stupidest questions I ever heard. She got a confused, disgusted look on her face, like she done salted her coffee instead a sugared it.

I turn back to my washing, so she don't see me rolling my eyes. "Oh no, ma'am, everthing's fine."

"But that talk in there, about the *bathroom*—" and smack on that word, Miss Leefolt walk in the kitchen.

"Oh, there you are, Skeeter." She look at us both kind a funny. "I'm sorry, did I... interrupt something?" We both stand there, wondering what she might a heard.

"I have to run," Miss Skeeter says. "See you tomorrow, Elizabeth." She open the back door, say, "Thanks, Aibileen, for lunch," and she gone.

I go in the dining room, start clearing the bridge table. And just like I knew she would, Miss Leefolt come in behind me wearing her upset smile. Her neck's sticking out like she fixing to ask me something. She don't like me talking to her friends when she ain't around, never has. Always wanting to know what we saying. I go right on past her into the kitchen. I put Baby Girl in her high chair and start cleaning the oven.

Miss Leefolt follow me in there, eyeball a bucket a Crisco, put it down. Baby Girl hold her arms out for her mama to pick her up, but Miss Leefolt open a cabinet, act like she don't see. Then she slam it close, open another one. Finally she just stand there. I'm down on my hands and knees. Pretty soon my head's so far in that oven I look like I'm trying to gas myself.

"You and Miss Skeeter looked like you were talking awful serious about something."

"No ma'am, she just…asking do I want some old clothes," I say and it sound like I'm down in a well-hole. Grease already working itself up my arms. Smell like a underarm in here. Don't take no time fore sweat's running down my nose and ever time I scratch at it, I get a plug a crud on my face. Got to be the worst place in the world, inside a oven. You in here, you either cleaning or you getting cooked. Tonight I just know I'm on have that dream I'm stuck inside and the gas gets turned on. But I keep my head in that awful place cause I'd rather be anywhere sides answering Miss Leefolt's questions about what Miss Skeeter was trying to say to me. Asking do I want to *change* things.

After while, Miss Leefolt huff and go out to the carport. I figure she looking at where she gone build me my new colored bathroom.

CHAPTER 2

Y OU'D NEVER KNOW IT living here, but Jackson, Mississippi, be filled with two hundred thousand peoples. I see
them numbers in the paper and I got to wonder, where do them
peoples live? Underground? Cause I know just about everbody
on my side a the bridge and plenty a white families too, and that
sure don't add up to be no two hundred thousand.

Six days a week, I take the bus across the Woodrow Wilson
Bridge to where Miss Leefolt and all her white friends live, in
a neighborhood call Belhaven. Right next to Belhaven be the
downtown and the state capital. Capitol building is real big,
pretty on the outside but I never been in it. I wonder what they
pay to clean that place.

Down the road from Belhaven is white Woodland Hills, then
Sherwood Forest, which is miles a big live oaks with the moss
hanging down. Nobody living in it yet, but it's there for when
the white folks is ready to move somewhere else new. Then it's
the country, out where Miss Skeeter live on the Longleaf cotton

plantation. She don't know it, but I picked cotton out there in 1931, during the Depression, when we didn't have nothing to eat but state cheese.

So Jackson's just one white neighborhood after the next and more springing up down the road. But the colored part a town, we one big anthill, surrounded by state land that ain't for sale. As our numbers get bigger, we can't spread out. Our part a town just gets thicker.

I get on the number six bus that afternoon, which goes from Belhaven to Farish Street. The bus today is nothing but maids heading home in our white uniforms. We all chatting and smiling at each other like we own it—not cause we mind if they's white people on here, we sit anywhere we want to now thanks to Miss Parks—just cause it's a friendly feeling.

I spot Minny in the back center seat. Minny short and big, got shiny black curls. She setting with her legs splayed, her thick arms crossed. She seventeen years younger than I am. Minny could probably lift this bus up over her head if she wanted to. Old lady like me's lucky to have her as a friend.

I take the seat in front a her, turn around and listen. Everbody like to listen to Minny.

"...so I said, Miss Walters, the world don't want a see your naked white behind any more than they want a see my black one. Now, get in this house and put your underpants and some clothes on."

"On the front porch? Naked?" Kiki Brown ask.

"Her behind hanging to her knees."

The bus is laughing and chuckling and shaking they heads.

"Law, that woman crazy," Kiki say. "I don't know how you always seem to get the crazy ones, Minny."

"Oh, like your Miss Patterson ain't?" Minny say to Kiki. "Shoot, she call the roll a the crazy lady club." The whole bus be laughing now cause Minny don't like nobody talking bad about her white lady except herself. That's her job and she own the rights.

The bus cross the bridge and make the first stop in the colored neighborhood. A dozen or so maids get off. I go set in the open seat next to Minny. She smile, bump me hello with her elbow. Then she relax back in her seat cause she don't have to put on no show for me.

"How you doing? You have to iron pleats this morning?"

I laugh, nod my head. "Took me a hour and a half."

"What you feed Miss Walters at bridge club today? I worked all morning making that fool a caramel cake and then she wouldn't eat a crumb."

That makes me remember what Miss Hilly say at the table today. Any other white lady and no one would care, but we'd all want a know if Miss Hilly after us. I just don't know how to put it.

I look out the window at the colored hospital go by, the fruit stand. "I think I heard Miss Hilly say something about that, bout her mama getting skinny." I say this careful as I can. "Say maybe she getting mal-nutritious."

Minny look at me. "She did, did she?" Just the name make her eyes narrow. "What else Miss Hilly say?"

I better just go on and say it. "I think she got her eye on you, Minny. Just...be extra careful around her."

"Miss Hilly ought to be extra careful around *me*. What she say, I can't cook? She say that old bag a bones ain't eating cause I can't feed her?" Minny stand up, throw her purse up on her arm.

"I'm sorry, Minny, I only told you so you stay out a her—"

"She ever say that to me, she gone get a piece a Minny for lunch." She huff down the steps.

I watch her through the window, stomping off toward her house. Miss Hilly ain't somebody to mess with. Law, maybe I should a just kept it to myself.

. . .

A COUPLE MORNINGS LATER, I get off the bus, walk the block to Miss Leefolt's house. Parked in front is a old lumber truck. They's two colored mens inside, one drinking a cup a coffee, the other asleep setting straight up. I go on past, into the kitchen.

Mister Raleigh Leefolt still at home this morning, which is rare. Whenever he here, he look like he just counting the minutes till he get to go back to his accounting job. Even on Saturday. But today he carrying on bout something.

"This is my damn house and I pay for what goddamn goes in it!" Mister Leefolt yell.

Miss Leefolt trying to keep up behind him with that smile that mean she ain't happy. I hide out in the washroom. It's been two days since the bathroom talk come up and I was hoping it was over. Mister Leefolt opens the back door to look at the truck setting there, slam it back closed again.

"I put up with the new clothes, all the damn trips to New Orleans with your sorority sisters, but this takes the goddamn cake."

"But it'll increase the value of the house. Hilly said so!" I'm still in the washroom, but I can almost hear Miss Leefolt trying to keep that smile on her face.

"We can't afford it! And we do not take orders from the Holbrooks!"

Everthing get real quiet for a minute. Then I hear the *pap-pap* a little feetum pajamas.

"Da-dee?"

I come out the washroom and into the kitchen then cause Mae Mobley's my business.

Mister Leefolt already kneeling down to her. He's wearing a smile look like it's made out a rubber. "Guess what, honey?"

She smile back. She waiting for a good surprise.

"You're not going to college so your mama's friends don't have to use the same bathroom as the maid."

He stomp off and slam the door so hard it make Baby Girl blink.

Miss Leefolt look down at her, start shaking her finger. "Mae Mobley, you know you're not supposed to climb up out of your crib!"

Baby Girl, she looking at the door her daddy slammed, she looking at her mama frowning down at her. My baby, she swallowing it back, like she trying real hard not to cry.

I rush past Miss Leefolt, pick Baby Girl up. I whisper, "Let's go on in the living room and play with the talking toy. What that donkey say?"

"She keeps getting up. I put her back in bed three times this morning."

"Cause somebody needs changing. Whooooweeee."

Miss Leefolt tisk, say, "Well I didn't realize..." but she already staring out the window at the lumber truck.

I go on to the back, so mad I'm stomping. Baby Girl been in that bed since eight o'clock last night, a course she need changing! Miss Leefolt try to sit in twelve hours worth a bathroom mess without getting up!

I lay Baby Girl on the changing table, try to keep my mad inside. Baby Girl stare up at me while I take off her diaper. Then she reach out her little hand. She touch my mouth real soft.

"Mae Mo been bad," she say.

"No, baby, you ain't been bad," I say, smoothing her hair back. "You been good. Real good."

I LIVE ON GESSUM AVENUE, where I been renting since 1942. You could say Gessum got a lot a personality. The houses all be small, but every front yard's different—some scrubby and grassless like a baldheaded old man. Others got azalea bushes and roses and thick green grass. My yard, I reckon it be somewhere in between.

I got a few red camellia bushes out front a the house. My grass be kind a spotty and I still got a big yellow mark where Treelore's pickup sat for three months after the accident. I ain't got no trees. But the backyard, now it looks like the Garden of Eden. That's where my next-door neighbor, Ida Peek, got her vegetable patch.

Ida ain't got no backyard to speak of what with all her husband's junk—car engines and old refrigerators and tires. Stuff he say he gone fix but never do. So I tell Ida she come plant on my side. That way I don't have no mowing to tend to and she let me pick whatever I need, save me two or three dollars ever week. She put up what we don't eat, give me jars for the winter season. Good turnip greens, eggplant, okra by the bushel, all kind a gourds. I don't know how she keep them bugs out a her tomatoes, but she do. And they good.

That evening, it's raining hard outside. I pull out a jar a Ida Peek's cabbage and tomato, eat my last slice a leftover cornbread. Then I set down to look over my finances cause two things done happen: the bus gone up to fifteen cents a ride and my rent gone up to twenty-nine dollars a month. I work for Miss Leefolt eight to four, six days a week except Saturdays. I get paid forty-three dollars ever Friday, which come to $172 a month. That means after I pay the light bill, the water bill, the gas bill, and the telephone bill, I got thirteen dollars and fifty cents a week left for my groceries, my clothes, getting my hair done, and tithing to the church. Not to mention the cost to mail these bills done gone up to a nickel. And my work shoes is so thin, they look like they starving to death. New pair cost seven dollars though, which means I'm on be eating cabbage and tomato till I turn into Br'er Rabbit. Thank the Lord for Ida Peek, else I be eating nothing.

My phone ring, making me jump. Before I can even say hello, I hear Minny. She working late tonight.

"Miss Hilly sending Miss Walters to the old lady home. I got to find myself a new job. And you know when she going? Next *week*."

"Oh *no*, Minny."

"I been looking, call ten ladies today. Not even a speck a interest."

I am sorry to say I ain't surprised. "I ask Miss Leefolt first thing tomorrow do she know anybody need help."

"Hang on," Minny say. I hear old Miss Walter talking and Minny say, "What you think I am? A chauffeur? I ain't driving you to no country club in the pouring rain."

Sides stealing, worse thing you'n do for your career as a maid is have a smart mouth. Still, she such a good cook, sometimes it makes up for it.

"Don't you worry, Minny. We gone find you somebody deaf as a doe-knob, just like Miss Walter."

"Miss Hilly been hinting around for me to come work for her."

"What?" I talk stern as I can: "Now you look a here, Minny, I support you myself fore I let you work for that evil lady."

"Who you think you talking to, Aibileen? A monkey? I might as well go work for the KKK. And you know I never take Yule May's job away."

"I'm sorry, Lordy me." I just get so nervous when it come to Miss Hilly. "I call Miss Caroline over on Honeysuckle, see if she know somebody. And I call Miss Ruth, she so nice it near bout break your heart. Used to clean up the house ever morning so I didn't have nothing to do but keep her company. Her husband died a the scarlet fever, mm-hmm."

"Thank you, A. Now come on, Miss Walters, eat up a little green bean for me." Minny say goodbye and hang up the phone.

. . .

THE NEXT MORNING, there that old green lumber truck is again. Banging's already started but Mister Leefolt ain't stomping around today. I guess he know he done lost this one before it even started.

Miss Leefolt setting at the kitchen table in her blue-quilt bathrobe talking on the telephone. Baby Girl's got red sticky all over her face, hanging on to her mama's knees trying to get her to look at her.

"Morning, Baby Girl," I say.

"Mama! Mama!" she say, trying to crawl up in Miss Leefolt's lap.

"No, Mae Mobley." Miss Leefolt nudge her down. "Mama's on the telephone. Let Mama talk."

"Mama, pick up," Mae Mobley whine and reach out her arms to her mama. "Pick Mae Mo up."

"Hush," Miss Leefolt whisper.

I scoop Baby Girl up right quick and take her over to the sink, but she keep craning her neck around, whining, "Mama, *Mama*," trying to get her attention.

"Just like you told me to say it." Miss Leefolt nodding into the phone. "Someday when we move, it'll raise the value of the house."

"Come on, Baby Girl. Put your hands here, under the water."

But Baby Girl wriggling hard. I'm trying to get the soap on her fingers but she twisting and turning and she snake right out my arms. She run straight to her mama and stick out her chin and then she jerk the phone cord hard as she can. The receiver clatter out a Miss Leefolt's hand and hit the floor.

"Mae Mobley!" I say.

I rush to get her but Miss Leefolt get there first. Her lips is curled back from her teeth in a scary smile. Miss Leefolt slap

Baby Girl on the back a her bare legs so hard I jump from the sting.

Then Miss Leefolt grab Mae Mobley by the arm, jerk it hard with ever word. "Don't you touch this phone again, Mae Mobley!" she say. "Aibileen, how many times do I have to tell you to keep her away from me when I am on the phone!"

"I'm sorry," I say and I pick up Mae Mobley, try to hug her to me, but she bawling and her face is red and she fighting me.

"Come on, Baby Girl, it's alright, everthing—"

Mae Mobley make an ugly face at me and then she rear back and *bowp*! She whack me right on the ear.

Miss Leefolt point at the door, yell, "Aibileen, you both just get *out*."

I carry her out the kitchen. I'm so mad at Miss Leefolt, I'm biting my tongue. If the fool would just pay her child some attention, this wouldn't happen! When we make it to Mae Mobley's room, I set in the rocking chair. She sob on my shoulder and I rub her back, glad she can't see the mad on my face. I don't want her to think it's at her.

"You okay, Baby Girl?" I whisper. My ear smarting from her little fist. I'm so glad she hit me instead a her mama, cause I don't know what that woman would a done to her. I look down and see red fingermarks on the back a her legs.

"I'm here, baby, Aibee's here," I rock and soothe, rock and soothe.

But Baby Girl, she just cry and cry.

AROUND LUNCHTIME, when my stories come on tee-vee, it gets quiet out in the carport. Mae Mobley's in my lap helping me string the beans. She still kind a fussy from this morning. I reckon I am too, but I done pushed it down to a place where I don't have to worry with it.

We go in the kitchen and I fix her baloney sandwich. In the driveway, the workmen is setting in they truck, eating they own lunches. I'm glad for the peace. I smile over at Baby Girl, give her a strawberry, so grateful I was here during the trouble with her mama. I hate to think what would a happen if I wasn't. She stuff the strawberry in her mouth, smile back. I think she feel it too.

Miss Leefolt ain't here so I think about calling Minny at Miss Walter, see if she found any work yet. But before I get around to it, they's a knock on the back door. I open it to see one a the workmen standing there. He real old. Got coveralls on over a white collar shirt.

"Hidee, ma'am. Trouble you for some water?" he ask. I don't recognize him. Must live somewhere south a town.

"Sho nuff," I say.

I go get a paper cup from the cupboard. It's got happy birthday balloons on it from when Mae Mobley turn two. I know Miss Leefolt don't want me giving him one a the glasses.

He drink it in one long swallow and hand me the cup back. His face be real tired. Kind a lonesome in the eyes.

"How y'all coming along?" I ask.

"It's work," he say. "Still ain't no water to it. Reckon we run a pipe out yonder from the road."

"Other fella need a drink?" I ask.

"Be mighty nice." He nod and I go get his friend a little funny-looking cup too, fill it up from the sink.

He don't take it to his partner right away.

"Beg a pardon," he say, "but where..." He stand there a minute, look down at his feet. "Where might I go to make water?"

He look up and I look at him and for a minute we just be looking. I mean, it's one a them funny things. Not the ha-ha funny but the funny where you be thinking: Huh. Here we is with two in the house and one being built and they still ain't no place for this man to do his business.

"Well..." I ain't never been in this position before. The young'un, Robert, who do the yard ever two weeks, I guess he go fore he come over. But this fella, he a old man. Got heavy wrinkled hands. Seventy years a worry done put so many lines in his face, he like a road map.

"I spec you gone have to go in the bushes, back a the house," I hear myself say, but I wish it weren't me. "Dog's back there, but he won't bother you."

"Alright then," he say. "Thank ya."

I watch him walk back real slow with the cup a water for his partner.

The banging and the digging go on the rest a the afternoon.

ALL THE NEXT DAY LONG, they's hammering and digging going on in the front yard. I don't ask Miss Leefolt no questions about it and Miss Leefolt don't offer no explanation. She just peer out the back door ever hour to see what's going on.

Three o'clock the racket stops and the mens get in they truck and leave. Miss Leefolt, she watch em drive off, let out a big sigh. Then she get in her car and go do whatever it is she do when she ain't nervous bout a couple a colored mens hanging round her house.

After while, the phone ring.

"Miss Leef—"

"She telling everbody in town I'm stealing! That's why I can't get no work! That witch done turned me into the Smart-Mouthed Criminal Maid a Hinds County!"

"Hold on, Minny, get your breath—"

"Before work this morning, I go to the Renfroes' over on Sycamore and Miss Renfroe near bout chase me off the property. Say Miss Hilly told her about me, everbody know I stole a candelabra from Miss Walters!"

I can hear the grip she got on the phone, sound like she trying to crush it in her hand. I hear Kindra holler and I wonder why Minny already home. She usually don't leave work till four.

"I ain't done nothing but feed that old woman good food and look after her!"

"Minny, I know you honest. God know you honest."

Her voice dip down, like bees on a comb. "When I walk into Miss Walters', Miss Hilly be there and she try to give me twenty dollars. She say, 'Take it. I know you need it,' and I bout spit in her face. But I didn't. No sir." She start making this panting noise, she say, "I did *worse*."

"What you did?"

"I ain't telling. I ain't telling nobody about that pie. But I give her what she deserve!" She wailing now and I feel a real cold fear. Ain't no game crossing Miss Hilly. "I ain't never gone get no work again, Leroy gone kill me . . ."

Kindra gets to crying in the background. Minny hang up without even saying goodbye. I don't know what she talking about a pie. But Law, knowing Minny, it could not have been good.

THAT NIGHT, I pick me a poke salad and a tomato out a Ida's garden. I fry up some ham, make a little gravy for my biscuit. My wig been brushed out and put up, got my pink rollers in, already sprayed the Good Nuff on my hair. I been worried all afternoon, thinking bout Minny. I got to put it out a my mind if I'm on get some sleep tonight.

I set at my table to eat, turn on the kitchen radio. Little Stevie Wonder's singing "Fingertips." Being colored ain't nothing on that boy. He twelve years old, blind, and got a hit on the radio. When he done, I skip over Pastor Green playing his sermon and stop on WBLA. They play the juke joint blues.

I like them smoky, liquor-drinking sounds when it get dark. Makes me feel like my whole house is full a people. I can almost see em, swaying here in my kitchen, dancing to the blues. When I turn off the ceiling light, I pretend we at The Raven. They's little tables with red-covered lights. It's May or June and warm. My man Clyde flash me his white-toothed smile and say *Honey, you want you a drink?* And I say, *Black Mary straight up* and then I get to laughing at myself, setting in my kitchen having this day-dream, cause the raciest thing I ever take is the purple Nehi.

Memphis Minny get to singing on the radio how lean meat won't fry, which is about how the love don't last. Time to time, I think I might find myself another man, one from my church. Problem is, much as I love the Lord, churchgoing man never do all that much for me. Kind a man I like ain't the kind that stays around when he done spending all you money. I made that mistake twenty years ago. When my husband Clyde left me for that no-count hussy up on Farish Street, one they call Cocoa, I figured I better shut the door for good on that kind a business.

A cat get to screeching outside and bring me back to my cold kitchen. I turn the radio off and the light back on, fish my prayer book out my purse. My prayer book is just a blue notepad I pick up at the Ben Franklin store. I use a pencil so I can erase till I get it right. I been writing my prayers since I was in junior high. When I tell my seventh-grade teacher I ain't coming back to school cause I got to help out my mama, Miss Ross just about cried.

"You're the smartest one in the class, Aibileen," she say. "And the only way you're going to keep sharp is to read *and write* every day."

So I started writing my prayers down instead a saying em. But nobody's called me smart since.

I turn the pages a my prayer book to see who I got tonight. A few times this week, I thought about maybe putting Miss Skeeter on my list. I'm not real sure why. She always nice when she come over. It makes me nervous, but I can't help but wonder what she was gone ask me in Miss Leefolt's kitchen, about do I want to change things. Not to mention her asking me the whereabouts a Constantine, her maid growing up. I know what happen between Constantine and Miss Skeeter's mama and ain't no way I'm on tell her that story.

The thing is though, if I start praying for Miss Skeeter, I know that conversation gone continue the next time I see her. And the next and the next. Cause that's the way prayer do. It's like electricity, it keeps things going. And the bathroom situation, it just ain't something I really want to discuss.

I scan down my prayer list. My Mae Mobley got the number one rung, then they's Fanny Lou at church, ailing from the rheumatism. My sisters Inez and Mable in Port Gibson that got eighteen kids between em and six with the flu. When the list be thin, I slip in that old stinky white fella that live behind the feed store, the one lost his mind from drinking the shoe polish. But the list be pretty full tonight.

And look a there who else I done put on this list. Bertrina Bessemer a all people! Everbody know Bertrina and me don't take to each other ever since she call me a nigga fool for marrying Clyde umpteen years ago.

"Minny," I say last Sunday, "why Bertrina ask *me* to pray for her?"

We walking home from the one o'clock service. Minny say, "Rumor is you got some kind a power prayer, gets better results than just the regular variety."

"Say what?"

"Eudora Green, when she broke her hip, went on your list, up walking in a week. Isaiah fell off the cotton truck, on your prayer list that night, back to work the next day."

Hearing this made me think about how I didn't even get the

chance to pray for Treelore. Maybe that's why God took him so fast. He didn't want a have to argue with me.

"Snuff Washington," Minny say, "Lolly Jackson—heck, Lolly go on your list and two days later she pop up from her wheelchair like she touched Jesus. Everbody in Hinds County know about that one."

"But that ain't me," I say. "That's just prayer."

"But Bertrina—" Minny get to laughing, say, "You know Cocoa, the one Clyde run off with?"

"Phhh. You know I never forget her."

"Week after Clyde left you, I heard that Cocoa wake up to her cootchie spoilt like a rotten oyster. Didn't get better for three months. Bertrina, she good friends with Cocoa. She *know* your prayer works."

My mouth drop open. Why she never tell me this before? "You saying people think I got the black magic?"

"I knew it make you worry if I told you. They just think you got a better connection than most. We all on a party line to God, but you, you setting right in his ear."

My teapot start fussing on the stove, bringing me back to real life. Law, I reckon I just go ahead and put Miss Skeeter on the list, but how come, I don't know. Which reminds me a what I don't want a think about, that Miss Leefolt's building me a bathroom cause she think I'm diseased. And Miss Skeeter asking don't I want to change things, like changing Jackson, Mississippi, gone be like changing a lightbulb.

from

How to Be an American Housewife

by

Margaret Dilloway

"This radiant debut pays moving tribute to the power of forgiveness." —*People*

When Shoko decided to marry an American GI and leave Japan, she had her parents' blessing, her brother's scorn, and a gift from her betrothed—a book titled How to Be an American Housewife. *As she crossed the ocean to America, Shoko also carried a secret she wanted to keep her entire life…*

Half a century later, Shoko's plans to finally return to Japan and reconcile with her brother are derailed by illness. Instead she sends her grown American daughter, Sue, a divorced single mother. As Sue takes in Japan, she also unearths Shoko's true story, and returns to America irrevocably touched, irrevocably changed…

Once you leave Japan, it is extremely unlikely that you will return, unless your husband is stationed there again or becomes wealthy.

Take a few reminders of Japan with you, if you have room. Or make arrangements to write to a caring relative who is willing to send you letters or items from your homeland. This can ease homesickness.

And be sure to tell your family, "Sayonara."

❖

—from the chapter "Turning American,"
in TAMIKO KELLY AND JUN TANAKA, *How to Be an American Housewife* (1955)

One

I had always been a disobedient girl.

When I was four, we lived in a grand house with a courtyard and a koi fishpond. My father worked as a lawyer and we were still rich, rich enough to have beautiful silk dresses and for me to have dolls with real hair and porcelain faces, not the corn-husk dolls I played with later.

We even had a nanny to help my mother. One day, Nanny told me she was taking my baby brother and me on a picnic. We walked for what seemed like miles, until my small feet were blistered. In those days, people expected more from a four-year-old than they do now.

"Where are we going?" I asked Nanny.

"To rest from the heat," she said. "By a pond."

I did not like Nanny. I didn't trust how she eyed my brother, Taro, like he was the last bowl of rice. She always hugged him tight, so tight he wailed, like she wanted to absorb him into her body. She had never had a son of her own, only daughters. Sometimes she called Taro "my little peach," like he was the peach boy out of the old fairy tale, granted as a wish to the old woman.

I told my mother that Nanny made me uncomfortable. She dismissed it as the whining of a spoiled child. "You don't like Nanny because she makes you behave," Mother said. "Now go with her. I have business in town, and your father is busy, too."

Nanny was old and had a crippled leg; she moved slowly. We stopped by a tree-shaded pond to play and have lunch. Afterward, in the high-noon heat, she took us under a willow tree to nap. Day turned to night. I awoke with a start to see the moon rising above the fields. "Where are we?" I asked.

"Shush," Nanny said soothingly, smoothing my bangs back. "We're going on a trip to my hometown." She looked down the road as though waiting for someone, or something. Her eyes glittered black onyx in the dim light. Taro began wailing and Nanny stuck a bottle into his mouth. "Go back to sleep, Shoko-chan."

Something was not right. We had missed supper. Mother didn't allow us to stay outside past dark. I stood. "You take us home right now!" I screamed.

"Sit down, sit down," Nanny said, trying to push on my shoulders. "You bad girl, listen to Nanny."

"No!" I kicked her in the shin as hard as I could, then pushed Taro's pram back up the road. I knew the way home, even though it was far.

Nanny's hand grabbed my arm and she lifted me up. Now she looked like a terrible witch, her wiry white hair free of her scarf, her jagged teeth bared like a wolf. "We're going on a trip. You must listen to Nanny!"

I bit her hand, bearing down hard in desperation. She yowled and dropped me. I stood up and pushed Taro away again.

This time she didn't follow. I looked back once and saw her standing in the middle of the road, holding her hand. Taro wailed.

Mother and Father were outside the wall of our house, looking left and right. They'd sent servants out looking for us. When they heard Taro, they ran to meet us. "Where have you been?" Mother cried, sweeping me up. Father cradled Taro to his face. Taro quieted.

"I told you she was no good!" I said, and recounted what had happened.

Some mothers would have not believed their child, but mine did. Mother said she had tried to steal us. Or, at the very least, steal my brother. Who knows what she would have done with me. "If it weren't for Shoko," Mother would retell visitors, shaking her head, *"Ai!"*

I was a hero. All because I wouldn't listen.

. . .

WITHIN A YEAR OR SO AFTER THAT, Father tired of dealing with bad people in his business. "Too much cheating," he told my mother. "All anyone cares about is money. Money is God."

He was always so busy. Perhaps he felt guilty that a nanny had almost made off with his children. He decided to sell the house and his practice and become a priest in the Konkokyo, the Konko Church.

In 1859, there was a Japanese village where people feared a god called Konjin, who brought misfortune. One farmer named Kawate Bunji had a streak of bad luck. Once when Bunji fell very ill, he was visited by the god Konjin, who told him that people shouldn't fear him, that he was good, and that his real name was Tenchi Kane no Kami, "One True God of Heaven and Earth." When Bunji became well, word of his visit from Konjin spread. People came to the farmer Bunji for help, and Tenchi Kane no Kami would speak through him. Bunji's name became Konkokyo Daijin, and he became a god, too. The Konko Church was born.

Mother never made a word of complaint when Father became a priest. Instead, she sold the house and all of our fine possessions, bargaining a more than fair price—"It goes to the church and brings you honor, what more could you wish?" she told the buyer. She let me keep one doll, my Shirley Temple with curly hair Father had bought in Tokyo, the one that melted later when I left it too close to the fireplace.

We moved to a tiny house with dirt floors covered by tatami mats. It was near the church in Ueki where my father would serve as priest. My sister, Suki, who was born that year, never knew a different life. I think that was why she was such a happy person. Or maybe it was because our parents never acted differently, rich or poor. Mother always made arrangements of flowers to brighten the room. We celebrated the festivals, with a little less feasting. Only I, with my memories of dolls and dresses, felt resentment.

Taro and I always played together. We were good friends until it began to bother Taro that I could hit a ball farther than he could, or climb a higher tree, or beat him in every race.

When Father decided I was too old to be a tomboy, around age thirteen, he made me take dance lessons, like all young ladies did. I did what my father told me to do. I was disobedient, not foolish. I learned how to flip open a fan with a flick of my wrist, peering over it at the audience. I also learned the shamisen, which was a little harp. The teacher said I was a beauty, and very talented. I didn't quite believe her until I saw how the men watched me at our talent show.

I came onstage in my beautiful silk kimono and red lips as my teacher played her shamisen. The bulbs shone in my eyes, but I would not squint. I lowered my gaze and snapped open my fan as I launched into the dance.

I heard an intake of breath from the men. I looked up and saw their admiring gazes fixed on me. I blushed, and kept on, knowing that wherever I went onstage their stares would follow. The other girls became invisible. I had more power in dance than I did at baseball.

I understood then that my skills in school or in sports would not make my life come about in the way I wished. I took my bows at that recital, vowing I would learn what I needed and make the best marriage possible.

THE WAR HAD CHANGED my life's direction from East to West. I heard about Pearl Harbor from my father. I was in third grade. Father, a priest in a religion that believed in peace, was worried. "America is so big," he fretted. "They will destroy us."

Mother reassured him. "If the Emperor says we will win, it will be fine. Japan is mighty."

Father seemed to be the only one around who questioned the Emperor. Everyone else thought we would triumph easily and show the West how strong we were. Even Father dared not bad-mouth the Emperor in public. The Emperor was supposed to be a god, and to say anything to the contrary could land you in prison.

At first, the war stayed far away, something we knew only from the radio. Then we began having blackouts and sirens. We built shelters in the hillsides to hide in when the planes came.

"Why would they bother with a countryside village, with no targets except chickens?" Father said.

But they did. One night, the alarms went off and we blacked out our windows so the planes wouldn't have easy targets. "It's just a drill," Father told us. We didn't bother to go out to the shelters.

But then we heard a great roar, the bombers overhead.

A blast rumbled the house. Something had been destroyed. At first light, I went outside. Our neighbor, Mrs. Miyama, and her little boy had been using their outhouse, and the light had been a beacon. Just like that, they were gone.

Another time, Taro, Suki, and I were walking to school. It was fall, the air just turning cold, the sky still gray. We had on our navy-blue-and-white school uniforms, our nice shoes that we could wear only to school. I remember that Taro's hair was slicked down as flat as Mother could get it.

Our road went through farmland, a country road with country people, nothing of any significance. Nothing that the Americans should bother with. Suddenly we heard the roar again. It was deafening. Suki stopped and clapped her hands over her ears. Father had told me what to do.

"Drop!" I ordered, pulling my sister to the ground and falling on top of her. Taro fell, too.

There were popping noises and the brown dirt in front of us lifted. We were being shot at. Three little children. I put my head down and prayed that we would be all right. The plane flew past and I started to get up.

The noise returned as the plane turned around. "It's coming back!" Taro yelled. He grabbed my arm, I grabbed Suki's arm, and we jumped over an embankment into an irrigation ditch at the side of the road. I looked up and saw the pilot and the plane as it came low. It had a star on its side, a skull and crossbones on the tail, and a half-naked woman painted near the front. The pilot saw me and laughed. He had been playing with us, scaring us. If he had wanted to, he could have killed us. That was the first time I ever saw an American.

Suki's face and body were muddy, and she was wailing. I took a chunk of mud out of her pigtails. Taro stood up and kicked at the dirt embankment, causing a slew of pebbles to fall down. He shook his fist toward the plane. "We will kill you all!" he shouted. "American fiends!"

I HAD NOT THOUGHT of this story for years.

I sat up on the couch in my San Diego living room, where I had been napping. Bright morning light made the room uncomfortably warm.

When I had told this story to my daughter, Sue, when she was still young enough to ask for stories, she had looked at me as if I were telling a grim fairy tale. "Why would they do that?" she had whispered, her eyes big.

"Those stories scare her," my husband, Charlie, had said. "The past is past."

He was right. And so I hardly talked about my past at all to my daughter. It was a lifetime ago. I had grown tired of my own stories, even of my old dreams. What good did dreams do me now? When you are young, dreams are the reason you pray for a new year and better luck.

Except for this. This one small dream of mine.

Taro and I together again.

I got a piece of tissue-thin airmail stationery and my husband's fountain pen out of the desk drawer. Sitting down on the floor at the coffee table, I put the pen to my lips, thinking. From the garage, Charlie sang as he put laundry in the washer. One of my adult son Mike's cats meowed at the screen door. I began my letter to Taro.

Many American husbands enjoy traditional aspects of Japanese culture, including the o-furo and the massage.

American husbands expect their Wives to be well-versed in massage as a Japanese tradition. Many men find that a small Japanese wife is an asset when she walks on his back after a long, tiring day.

Often when a Japanese person begins consuming Western foods, they become fat. Do not overindulge. It is important to keep oneself at a light enough weight so that the husband's back is uninjured.

The o-furo may also be enjoyed by your husband. Offering to scrub his back as you would with a Japanese spouse is likely to be welcomed. It is a small piece of service you may offer to him.

—from the chapter "A Map to Husbands,"
How to Be an American Housewife

Two

I carried the letter into my bedroom, pushing the door shut with my shoulder. We had lived here for over thirty years, and still this bedroom door was not fixed. I looked about for a place to hide the letter. Not that my husband, Charlie, was nosy, but he always thought of reasons to say no to me.

I stuck the note into my underwear drawer in the dresser. I met the eyes of the two Japanese samurai dolls in their glass case on top of the bureau. The man had a sword, and the girl had a tiny metal knife tucked into her kimono sleeve. A secret weapon no one saw. Underneath their case I had a secret of my own.

I opened the little glass door and lifted out the dolls, then lifted up a hidden compartment. Inside that was my *hesokuri*, my secret money. I'd been pinching pennies all these years. Stealing out of Charlie's change jar, saving bits of our tax refunds and Charlie's Navy retirement checks. Now I had a lot. Enough to go to Japan. I touched the cash and smiled.

Then I opened my closet to decide what to wear to see my cardiologist, Dr. Cunningham. Lately, I had been seeing him too much, getting tests and medications. My heart was giving out, and other things along with it. Last summer, I'd gotten Bell's palsy, paralyzing my face's right side for a week. I got a patch, like a pirate, so my eye wouldn't dry out. People crossed the street when they saw me coming. Once, they would have crossed the street to look at me.

"I ugly now," I said to Charlie more than once, just to hear him tell me I was beautiful.

He didn't disappoint. "You're beautiful still, Shoko."

"Why this happen?" I asked.

"No one knows," he said. "Only God."

Only God. I prayed to *kamisama*, not God, as my parents had raised me. I sighed and took out a pair of slacks I had worn the previous week, wondering if Dr. Cunningham would recognize them.

Unlike many of the new doctors at Balboa Naval Medical Center, where the doctors who just graduated from medical school go for training, Dr. Cunningham seemed to know what was going on.

I liked Dr. Cunningham. He looked just like Tyrone Power, a movie star I had loved when I was young. And he was single! If I had been young and single, I could have gotten him for sure. When I was in my teens, I'd been the prettiest girl around. High defined cheekbones, Cupid's bow of a full mouth, shiny blue-black hair, and pale white skin, like a baby's. I had an hourglass shape even with no girdle—a full bust, tiny waist (twenty-two inches), and womanly bottom. Men chased me from the time I turned twelve. And I enjoyed it, though being a nice girl, I shouldn't have.

My own daughter was as enchanting, if not more so. She didn't have short Japanese legs like I did. Her limbs were long and lean, her neck and fingers graceful. Eurasians were exotic, and men liked that, too. Sue could have had anyone, if she'd only waited for college before finding a husband, instead of marrying the first boy who came along. Which did not last, as I knew it would not.

I said to Dr. Cunningham, "My daughter could marry anyone, you know. Rich businessman love her."

And then Dr. Cunningham said, "If she's half as lovely as you, Mrs. Morgan, I'm missing out." He was so nice!

I picked up the phone by the bed now and dialed Sue's cell phone, hoping she wouldn't see my number and let it go to voice mail. I held my breath, waiting. She picked up. "What's up, Mom?" She sounded artificially cheerful. I imagined her sitting at her desk, twirling her dark brown hair around one finger, her pale face greenish in the light from her computer screen.

"Suiko-chan. You wanna take me doctor today?" I asked. "Got appointment after lunchtime."

I heard her carefully repressed sigh. "Is Dad busy?"

"Don't know. Maybe so." I couldn't tell her that Charlie had taken me yesterday and the day before that. I didn't want to worry her.

"I have a meeting, Mom." Sue was a manager at a financial services firm. Her voice turned brisk. "Are you still trying to get me to meet your doctor?"

I was glad she couldn't see the surprise on my face. If I could have, I would have chosen a husband for Sue. Sue needed someone already established, who had done all the hard work already. She needed someone to take care of her, so the dark circles under her eyes would go away.

Dr. Cunningham would be perfect. But in America, they find husbands themselves. I had found Charlie myself, almost American-style, and maybe I would have done things differently if I could go back.

"He's not interested, Mom," Sue said, her voice so flat it made my heart ache even more. "He's being polite. What's he supposed to say? Don't bother the man."

"But you need *see* this guy. If I you, I grab him up! Single doctor won't last long." I tried to keep my voice light, but my daughter didn't understand. A single doctor really wouldn't last long.

Sue snorted. "Mom, please. I can find my own man."

But she couldn't.

I heard what she was saying. *Stay out of my life.* I sat for a moment in silence. *I am writing a letter to your uncle now,* I wanted to tell her. *I am going to Japan. Don't you want to know?* I wanted to tell her so much more.

Dr. Cunningham had told me my heart was getting flabby, which meant it wasn't working well. He wanted me to have surgery with a specialist. They would cut a wedge out and make it smaller. "It's risky, but not as risky as a transplant," he had said.

"Fine," I had said. It took them months to schedule anything. I'd be to Japan and back before the first pre-op appointment.

"Is there something else, Mom?" Sue was trying to sound patient but not succeeding.

I tried to think quickly of something that would make her want to come with me. My daughter was too sensitive, too fast to hear criticism. Perhaps it was partially my fault.

I did not have the knack of subtlety. When she was a college sophomore, Sue had come to me while I was in my bedroom one afternoon. She squeaked the door closed, her face so pale, even in the golden light coming in from the west, that I thought she was ill. She sat on my side of the bed, next to the photo of my parents. "What's a matter you, Suiko-chan?" I asked her.

"Craig and I are going to move in together," she whispered.

I was shocked. I shouted at her. "You do that," I said, "and we no pay college no more! You bring shame on us." In my town, my family would never have been able to show their faces again if I had done something so scandalous.

Sue had looked around. "Shame from whom? We don't have any family here. The neighbors don't care." The afternoon sun made her hair glint red. "Besides, you're hardly paying anything. I have a ton of loans."

"I no can hold my head up." I was really hoping this would make her ditch Craig.

She had sighed. Nineteen years old, she was at the peak of her beauty. She thought her beauty would go on forever. The way I thought mine would. She needed to find someone better while she still could. "Then it's Plan B. We're getting married."

"Marry?" I closed my eyes and changed my tactics. My lovely daughter could not marry this person, the first boy she'd ever kissed. I had told her that you should only kiss if you were going to get married, but that was to keep her from being a slut. I never thought she'd take it so seriously. "Why you gonna marry same guy you drag around high school? That's why we send college. Find good man marry."

"There's nothing wrong with Craig." Sue's voice rose in anger.

She was right. There was nothing wrong with him. Except he would make a lousy husband. Too flighty, too artistic. High-maintenance. Maybe in twenty years he'd be ready. "Sue," I pleaded.

"Don't worry. I'll be out of your hair in a week," she spat, leaving the house. "I won't shame you anymore." The next weekend, she was in Vegas. Too young to drink but old enough to get married. And to have a baby.

I never said a bad word about Craig again, no matter what he did or how he acted.

Sue thought differently than I did, and I didn't understand her. Sometimes I thought I had chased her out of the house too soon, been too hard on her the way I had been too easy on her brother. It seemed both parenting methods had failed.

On the line with my daughter, I heard another beep. "Mom, my boss is calling me," Sue said. "Is there anything else you needed?"

It wasn't the right time to tell her everything. Not on the phone. "Go, then." I hung up. I suspected her boss wasn't on the phone, that she was simply tired of listening to her old mother. But she couldn't keep the honcho waiting.

I got dressed. In my bedroom, I had crammed pieces of Japan everywhere, all covered up. There was a hand-painted folding screen by the closet, wrapped in black trash bags. Scrolls and fans were in boxes in the closet. I didn't want anything to be ruined by the light, not until I could take them out again. When the kids took their junk out of the other bedrooms, I would make a Japanese room.

These things used to be displayed, treasured. When Charlie first brought me from Japan to Norfolk, I decorated our home to the best of my ability, with my Japanese furniture that Charlie and I had taken equal delight in picking out and that the Navy had shipped over: the Japanese screen painted with a waterfall and peacocks; ink-painted scrolls; statues of badgers and lions; and silk satin floor cushions I'd made. We had a sofa, too, but no one used it. With Mike a baby, the floor was more convenient.

Once a week, I'd go to the park and clip whatever foliage and flowers

I could find, arranging them in the Japanese way on the sideboard. A tall piece, a medium-size piece, and a small, all designed to suggest nature.

We had lived in a small two-bedroom town house with floors so crooked, you could roll a Coke can from one end to the other. Charlie was getting ready to ship out for at least a year, and it would be just me and the baby.

Charlie's relatives lived in Maryland, and they came to visit a few times. His mother, Millie, a stout woman who had borne eight children in ten years, was so encouraging that I thought all Americans would be like her. "Don't you marry her and then get rid of her like everybody else," she took Charlie aside and warned. Many Japanese women who married servicemen got abandoned when they got to the States and they found out how hard it was to live in a biracial marriage. Even more got left back in Japan, pregnant and unmarried.

"Don't worry," Charlie said.

"You call if you need anything, and I'll get someone to take me here," his mother said every time she left.

"Yes, Mother." I knew I would never bother her.

When she visited, she would bring me practical things, like boxes of tissue or a frying pan. I was grateful, but not when she looked around our small apartment.

It was different from her house, where nobody took off their shoes and they would rather use bricks and boards for shelving than spend money on furniture, and the only decorations were pictures of Jesus. If she had flowers, she stuck them all in a vase so big you couldn't see the other person at the table.

"This is all so fancy," Millie said every time she visited, trying to understand but not succeeding.

This way of living was the only way I knew. I couldn't live in a space without having something lovely to look at. Even when my parents were poor, they could still trim a pine bush outside into a bonsai. I imagined Millie went home and talked about how Charlie's wife spent all his money on unimportant clutter.

Charlie enjoyed Japanese art, though. I tried to teach him *sumi-e* brush painting, but no matter how much he practiced, his paintings looked like rudimentary stick figures. "How you get a few strokes to look like a deer—you're a genius," he said to me.

I only knew what a "genius" was from his awed tone. "Try again."

"There's only room for one genius here." He had three of my paintings matted and framed, and they hung in a trio on the wall.

Adjusting to the U.S. was difficult in other ways for me, especially in the beginning. If I borrowed an egg from a neighbor, I returned two, the Japanese way. They didn't understand; why did I give them two? It made them angry, like I was insulting them. When you "borrowed" an egg or a cup of sugar in America, you never actually returned it. Charlie had to explain: "It's her tradition."

"Never heard of a tradition like that," our neighbors said.

When Charlie wasn't home to explain my odd ways to people, I went to the store alone, with Mike bundled up in a thousand layers in his stroller. I made sure to dress up. My favorite outfit was a pencil skirt, button-up black blouse with white pipe trim, and heels. It wasn't the most comfortable thing to take care of a child in, but I was young and didn't care. I wanted to look presentable, not like a maid or a Jap with buckteeth and wild hair, but an American girl.

As I walked the two blocks from housing to the store, people stopped and stared, whispering, "There goes that Jap wife!" I smiled and waved, even when mothers held their children against them. A few of them stopped me, said hello, wanted to touch my hair, so much coarser than theirs. "Like horsehair!" they exclaimed.

I reminded myself that the Japanese had done the same thing with Charlie and his fire-red hair. "There goes the demon!" they had whispered. Certainly I could take it.

I kept my head high and said, "Hello!" I had practiced my *l* sounds in the mirror before I ever left Japan. It didn't matter whether people said hello back or not. I was holding up my end. What they did was their own business.

. . .

I SWUNG MY LEGS up onto the bed and massaged my ankle, wishing I could run for miles, like Sue could. I remembered how it felt not to get winded. When I was a kid, I had been a real tomboy. "Stay inside, Shoko," Father had said to me. "Your skin will get dark."

But I loved to play baseball, and I hit the ball better than the boys. I still loved baseball today. I watched every game I could on television, making Charlie grumble. He hated sports. I hated being indoors, but now allergies and the sun bothered me too much to spend time outside.

Once, when I was little, I sneaked out to the field where my brother played ball with his friends. "Go home and do the laundry, Shoko," Taro yelled at me when he saw me. His friends laughed and Taro drew himself up taller than he was, which was still half a head shorter than me. His black hair poked out crazily from under his ball cap; Taro had an unfortunate double-helix cowlick on the crown of his head. "We don't want girls messing up our game."

I couldn't let my little brother speak that way to me, especially in front of his older friend, Tetsuo, who always looked at me in a sly way and winked. I squared my shoulders. "I bet you your *manju* that I hit a home run." Our mother was making the steamed sweet bean cakes. Treats were getting fewer these days, so this was a bet of the utmost seriousness.

Of course I did hit a homer. Tetsuo and the other boys hooted and hollered. And Taro ran home and told our father, who beat me with a willow stick. "For being better than a boy?" I had shouted at him as he did it.

"For disobedience," Father had said, giving me an extra whack for talking back. Father, a tall and skinny scholar with glasses falling down his nose, hardly had the heart to give me a good beating. He did it only because it was the right thing for a father to do when a daughter ran wild.

Worst of all, he gave Taro my *manju*. But that night, after everyone had gone to sleep, I'd been awakened by a soft prodding on my cheek and the smell of sweet beans at my nose. "Here, Shoko-chan," Taro had whispered. "I'm sorry." He had given me two, his and mine.

"You better be sorry," I had responded, stuffing both into my cheeks. "I'll really fix you next time." I punched his arm. Taro giggled, and we drifted to sleep, the *manju* beans making my lips sticky.

Was Taro even still alive?

If you are lucky enough to become a mother to a son, do not attempt to raise him in the American way. Raise him in the Japanese way and he will become a fine young man in the Japanese tradition.

This means treating him better than you treat your husband. Prepare all your son's favorite meals, buy him toys when he desires them, try to accommodate all his desires before he can voice them. In this way, you will gain his respect and appreciation.

✖

—from the chapter "American Family Habits,"
How to Be an American Housewife

Three

Charlie interrupted my memories by coming in and patting my shin. "You want me to bring you Sanka in here?"

I sat up, then lay back down. How idiotic that the simple act of getting dressed had tired me out. Some days were better than others. "Please."

"Okay." He got up and left before I could mention my letter.

I stretched, thinking about how I would run after I got my heart fixed, then got up and applied my makeup. I only wore it to the store or to the doctor's, really the only places we ever went anymore.

Loud TV came out of my son's room, which was across from ours. I smelled cigarettes. My chest tightened. I went out and pounded on his door. "No smoke in house, Mike!"

He cracked the door open, his nearly black eyes rimmed with red. There were so many papers and trash and clothes on the floor you couldn't see the carpet. At the foot of his bed was a big-screen TV, up too loud. "What?" he said, like when he was sixteen, me trying to get him to come out for dinner, when he'd rather eat in his room alone. This was Mike's way.

Mike looked much more Japanese than Sue. He had sharp high cheekbones, eyes that turned up at the corners. His nose had a flat bridge like my brother's, but was long like his father's. Ever since he was little, wherever we went, people had stared at his Asian eyes, his sharp cheekbones, and his coarse black hair. He looked like the star of an old samurai movie, out of place in this time. I told him to stick his tongue out at them.

Maybe that was why he preferred the company of animals. Everywhere we moved, he had fish and a lizard. I wouldn't let him have cats and dogs until after we were done with our overseas tours, so we wouldn't have to give them up.

Moving so much for the Navy had been hard for Mike. It took him about two and a half years to make a good friend, and three years was how long each duty station lasted. When we left Washington state, Mike was six. He had sat down in the doorway of our old Craftsman bungalow and held on to the doorjamb, rocking himself back and forth while the movers hauled off our belongings, while his little friend Jimmy came to say good-bye, and his father and I packed the car. Five hours total. Nothing would budge him. "I'm staying. I like it."

I tried to pick him up. "Come on. We miss plane."

His fingernails left grooves in the wood, and he screeched. It sounded like a bald eagle getting shot down. He banged his head on the doorjamb.

"You hurt self! Stop!" I tried to block him and he gave me a tremendous slap on the arm. I backed off.

"Cut it out, Mike." Charlie put the last piece of luggage in the car and turned around, his face reddening in anger. "Get over here right now."

"I'll run away." Mike looked up at me. His face was sweaty and tear-stained. A bright red gash and a purple bruise were starting to appear. I bent to touch it and he jerked away.

I looked at my husband. Charlie wiped his brow, then sat down next to him and put his arm around him. "Mike, Daddy's getting time off after we move. I'll take you fishing in Guam. You won't believe the fish they have there. And the water's so warm. You can swim every day." Charlie always made the most of his leave time, taking Mike camping and fishing and giving me a break to be alone.

"But Jimmy's not there."

"You can write."

He glared at his father. "I don't know how."

Charlie ignored that. "Listen. This is how life is, Mike, and you have to adjust." Charlie stood up. "Get in the car."

He held on to the doorjamb. "No."

Charlie looked at Mike, then at me. "Fine. Get in the car, Shoko."

I did.

Charlie turned the ignition on and drove away quickly.

"What you doing?" I cried, looking back at my son. Mike's mouth was open in a wail.

"Teaching him a lesson for throwing a tantrum."

I turned, wondering if Mike would run to the neighbor's, if he would run down the driveway after us. Mike was still holding on to the house.

We drove to the end of the block, then turned around. Mike was still on the doorstep, his hands now in his lap, his face covered by new tears.

"I thought you left me," he said, hiccuping.

"We never leave you." I tried to put my arms around him. He pushed me off.

He stared. I saw that he did not believe me.

"You ready now?" Charlie asked him.

He went silently to the car, his head hanging down. Mike was too easily broken. What other children shrugged off, Mike could not. I shook my head at Charlie and got in the backseat next to my son. Charlie drove us silently to the airport.

Mike never complained about moving again. Instead he would sit in a corner, a blanket pulled over his head, shutting out us and the rest of the world, until I took him by the hand and led him to the car.

I stared at him now, an adult leaning against his doorjamb, seeing the little boy. "The smoke hurt my heart."

"What's the problem? I've got the window open." He cleared his throat. I hoped he wouldn't get lung cancer.

A black cat ran into the hallway. "Shoot." Mike had just gotten a notice to get out of his old place. Over the years, Mike had moved out and back more times than I could count. This time, he moved back in with four cats. They peed all over the living room. I put my foot down.

Now he kept them in his room, taking out the window screen so they could come in and out as they liked. But we were near a mountain, and coyotes had eaten two in the last week.

Mike slammed his door shut, chasing the cat. I leaned against the wall. He caught it in the living room and brought it back, cradled in his arms like a baby.

I crossed my arms. "You pay Daddy first month rent?"

Mike shrugged, pushing back his long hair with one hand. He went in his room and returned with a hundred-dollar bill, handing it to me without a word.

"How work going?" Mike had begun a new job at a pet store.

He shrugged again, and his eyes flicked back toward his closed door like he was missing his favorite show. "Fine."

"Maybe you go back school, be a vet? You like that. Never too late." I would go back to school, if I could. Grossmont Community College was only a mile away.

"Maybe. Yeah."

I knew he only said that to make me shut up. "No more smoke room. Outside only."

"Fine." He was barely listening, his head cocked toward the television dialogue.

I wanted to tell him more: that he needed to clean the filthy bathroom he used; that he should rinse out his dishes; that he should keep his room neat. It was no use. If he cleaned the bathroom, first I'd have to nag, and then he'd do a halfway bad job at it, so I would have to redo it anyway. It was easier for me or Charlie to do, even with our ailments.

"You have dinner with us?" I asked him.

He shrugged.

"What mean? Say yes, say no. No shrug."

"No, then." He shuffled his feet.

"Got work?"

"Yeah." The cat in his arms purred. He put his nose to its nose.

"You not watch so much TV. Make brain Jell-O. Read book." I scratched the cat's neck. It licked my hand, sandpapery wet.

"Okay." Mike opened his door and disappeared inside.

I wondered if we should keep letting him move back in. After all, he was fifty. But he still hadn't married. And who would ever marry him?

I raised him like my mother had raised my brother. By doing everything for him. I knew no better. I had hoped he would still grow up to be a hard worker. Japanese boys turn out fine raised like this, but apparently not Americans. Or not my son.

When Mike was a toddler and we lived in Virginia, I'd take him to the park and try to meet other children for playmates. For both of us.

Children that young—Mike was a year and a half—didn't care what a child looked like. Their mothers did. "He doesn't look the least bit American," one mother remarked to me as our sons dug sand near each other. "He really takes after you."

The mothers varied from polite to downright cold. I couldn't blame them. Some had lost their fathers in the war with Japan. But I felt they could afford to be a little forgiving, seeing as how we lost in the end. Especially the manner in which we lost.

Time did not make our way smoother. When Mike was twelve and playing Little League in Oakland, all the mothers had to make treats for their end-of-season party. Mike had told me about it as I sat on the bleachers watching the game, by myself, on the top row. "It's tomorrow," he said, throwing the ball into his mitt and not looking at me.

The other mothers sat a few rows down or clumped in groups of two or three. They wore button-down shirts in pastel colors and capri pants, like a secret uniform. "Why they no tell me?" I asked.

He shrugged and asked for snack money. I gave him a quarter and moved two benches down to Jackie, the team mother. Jackie had dark hair and a flip just like Jackie O, whom she resembled. She wore a giant floppy straw hat.

Jackie smiled politely and I back at her. "Hi, Shoko, how are you?"

"Very well, thank you." I used my softest, most pleasant voice. "Jackie. I bring popacor-nu barus to party."

"What's that?" Jackie said, not moving her lips from the smile.

"Popacor-nu barus."

She blinked. "I'm sorry. One more time?"

"Popacor-nu. Barus." I made the shape with my hands.

Jackie was silent, her head cocked to the side, the smile fading. The other mothers watched. Did they not understand, either?

Mike had come back and was standing in the dirt by the bleachers, watching. "It's popcorn balls!" he shouted. "What the hell is so hard to understand? You people are stupid. This team is stupid." He threw his hat down.

I never went to another game. But neither did I cry about it. Mike did not, either, or if he did, he did not let us know.

I sorrowed for Mike. He had not changed much from the little boy on the front stoop. Less fussy, yes. But still easily broken. No one had ever been able to understand him. Always, he was moody, a loner, smart as a whip but lazy. Often he was in his own world, amusing himself. Today, Charlie said Mike might have been called "mildly autistic," but not when he was growing up. Back then, he was just different, and we had done the best we could.

I only hoped that Charlie would let Mike keep staying here after I was gone. He had nowhere else to go.

CHARLIE CAME DOWN THE HALL, a mug of Sanka in his hands. "You want to have spaghetti tonight?"

"No, no," I murmured. "We out of noodle." I considered telling Charlie about the letter right then. Perhaps he would have advice. *Our dear Suki has passed on,* I had written thus far. *Perhaps it is time for us to make amends . . .* Only last week, my sister's husband had sent word that Suki had passed on months ago, from the same condition I had. Her heart. There was no explanation for why he had waited so long to tell me. I was out here in the West, as forgotten as a ghost.

"I'll fry us some steaks. Better take them out of the freezer." Charlie hummed as he went into the bedroom and began putting away laundry.

"I cook tonight. Your steak dry."

He laughed. "I'll make yours bloody." He folded and sang.

Charlie had taken over most of the cooking. On days when I was tired, he pan-fried meat and made rice with microwaved frozen vegetables. Nothing like what I could make. I was just glad to have someone cook for me. Otherwise, we'd be eating cold cereal.

I hadn't always been a good cook. I had made spaghetti for Charlie for the first time in 1955, in that Norfolk house.

The spaghetti recipe was in the new American cookbook that Charlie gave me, *How to Be an American Housewife*. Written in Japanese and in English, it also taught the American way of housekeeping. I had never imagined that I would need such a book, since my mother and my high school had prepared me for being an excellent wife, but I had to admit, American ways were different. I took the book very seriously and made the spaghetti exactly as it said.

The spaghetti recipe had worked. I cooked all day long, using tomatoes I grew in our little garden. The tomatoes were huge that year—our cat Miki used the garden as a litterbox, and I also composted bits and pieces of kitchen scraps.

With Mike wrapped up on my back in a long bolt of material, I used all the strange ingredients we didn't have in Japan—sugar, bay leaf, basil, oregano, sage. "Everything in Japan tastes fishy," Charlie once told me, "even the spaghetti."

"Then why like sushi?" I asked.

"That's not fishy," he said.

That made no sense, so I threw my hands up.

I made certain not to use any fish sauce or soy sauce in this dish, though either would have made it taste a lot better. Then I let it simmer all day, just like it said to, wondering when my new husband would get home. The Navy mostly kept him on a regular schedule when he was ashore, but you never knew for sure. A military wife knew her husband doesn't truly belong to her.

When I heard Charlie singing up the walkway, I put the plate on the table and waited. I hadn't even eaten myself, though it was nearly seven o'clock. Mike was already asleep in the dresser drawer we had pulled out and padded as a temporary crib, swaddled in a receiving blanket I had knitted myself.

"*Tadaima!*" Charlie sang out the traditional Japanese greeting. I'm home.

"*Okaeri!*" I responded. Welcome back.

"Boy, it's too quiet in here." He hung his sailor hat by the door, his curly red hair popping up, and left his shiny black shoes next to my pumps. Then he turned on the television. "I'm going to look at Mike for a minute." Charlie headed for the bedroom. He loved that boy; he'd wake him up to hear his voice coo.

"No. You crazy? Never go back sleep." I blocked the doorway. "Eat."

He kissed me with a laugh, spinning me around so the collar on his dark sailor's uniform flew out. "Yes, madame." He scraped the metal chair out from the table and swung his leg over it, cowboy style. Then he tasted the spaghetti. I held my breath. He made a face. "Too sweet."

I sat down, trying to think of the English words. I shook my head and raised my hands. "What mean?"

"It's not like my mother's." He pushed the plate away. "I don't like the onion chunks."

His mother's sauce had most certainly been watered-down tomato paste and sugar, with no spices because they were poor. I stood up so quickly that the little wooden table slid away from me. "No eat, I throw!" I pointed at his head.

"What?" His lips twitched, trying not to smile.

"I throw." I picked up the plate. I saw that on television once. That was how I spent most of my time in America, watching television and learning English. On one show, the wife threw the dinner at the husband's face. "This from book." I shook my head. "No throw out." I would never really throw food at Charlie. I only wanted his attention. I never wasted food. In Japan, we never wasted a grain of rice or a speck of salt.

Charlie's eyes were big. I thought about our wedding day, when I wore a tall headdress. Some people said it was to cover up the woman's horns that showed up after marriage. That's what my father told Charlie, who had laughed. I wondered if Charlie was thinking about that, too, thinking that my horns were showing.

"All right, already," he said, putting a forkful into his mouth. He stared at the TV, like he always did. He used to watch it until two or three every night, even when there was nothing good on. And then he ate the entire plate, with seconds. As he should have. It was delicious, worth all my effort.

I had spent most of the previous day searching for the spices in the Commissary, the discount grocery store on the base where we bought our food. It was a marvel unlike anything else I'd seen in America so far, including the Statue of Liberty. There were gleaming aisles of every type of food you could dream of. In Japan, especially during the war, the storekeepers only had a few bags of rice. Salt. Some roots. Here, I wanted to buy everything and nothing. I didn't know how to cook the big juicy steaks Charlie loved; mine turned out leather dry. I had no idea how to make soup without miso or fish stock. I used water instead, and it tasted awful.

Day after day, I experimented with American foods from the Commissary, learning how to cook all over again. Fry up a piece of meat, boil potatoes, carefully reading the recipes in my book over and over. It was hard learning recipes from a book, all alone, with new ingredients. Sometimes I misread them, mixing up "baking powder" and "baking soda" more than once.

My own mother had taught me how to cook by observation. No formal measurements. Learning how to cook was like learning a language. You picked it up. All I had to do was be around her while she made rice or *manju* or fish stock, and just like that, I knew how to make these things, too.

From the time I first had memories, my mother had been teaching me how to be a good housewife. I helped her do the chores every day, cooking and cleaning and sewing. As we worked, she would sing. Usually she sang *isobushi*, meaning "rocky-beach melody," in her high, thin voice. It was one of the oldest folk songs, the same song fishermen and Noh actors had performed. It sounded like wailing, a lament.

Mother was tough; she came from farming peasant stock. She had a long torso, short powerful legs, and wide feet. The type of person who could squat in a field like a salaryman sat at a desk. Her hair had been half gray since I could remember. Her kimonos were darker colors, solid blues and reds flecked with white.

"Shoko-chan," she would say, "take this for me." I would take over stirring the pot of vegetables while she shifted my little sister Suki from her back to her front to nurse. In those days, children got nursed for a long time, until age two or three or even older. Sometimes that was all of the nourishment they got. It certainly was for my sister.

I watched my mother, her weariness etched on her face though her voice soared, her breasts two sad sacks of rice, and her song seemed more like a warning to me.

WHEN I HAD MY OWN DAUGHTER, I had tried to teach her how to cook, but Sue was a clumsy child. Nervous.

Once, at age seven or so, she made cookies with me. "Measure flour. Make flat with knife," I said to her. She spilled the flour all over immediately, then the sugar on the floor, then stuck a finger up her nose as she stood there, almost crying. I couldn't believe it. When I was seven, I was cooking and going to the shops alone, and my child couldn't even measure flour or tie a shoe.

"You watch, okay? Sit watch."

She had sat with a sad face on the chair.

"When old, no spill, you can help, okay?" I felt bad for her, but I did not have the time or energy to redo what she had done.

Now I realized I was too impatient. I should have taught her how to clean up. I should have shown her what to do as my mother had for me. Maybe that was why Sue could not learn my own *isobushi*, hear my own warning.

from

My Name Is Mary Sutter

by

Robin Oliveira

**"A vivid, dramatic novel about love, medicine,
and the Civil War, *My Name Is Mary Sutter* features
an indomitable, memorable heroine whom the
reader will root for until the very end."**

—David Ebershoff, author of *The 19th Wife* and *The Danish Girl*

*Mary Sutter is a brilliant young midwife who dreams of
becoming a surgeon. Determined to overcome the prejudices
against women in medicine—and eager to run away from
recent heartbreak—Mary travels to Washington, D.C.,
to help tend the legions of Civil War wounded. Under the
guidance of two surgeons, who both fall unwittingly in love
with her, and resisting her mother's pleas to return home
to help with the difficult birth of her twin sister's baby,
Mary pursues her medical career against all odds. Rich
with historical detail—including cameo appearances by
Abraham Lincoln and Dorothea Dix, among others—and
introducing a heroine whose unwavering determination and
vulnerability will resonate with readers everywhere,* My
Name Is Mary Sutter *is certain to be recognized as one of
the great novels of the Civil War.*

Chapter One

∿ "Are you Mary Sutter?" Hours had passed since James Blevens had called for the midwife. All manner of shouts and tumult drifted in from the street, and so he had answered the door to his surgery rooms with some caution, but the young woman before him made an arresting sight: taller and wider than was generally considered handsome, with an unflattering hat pinned to an unruly length of curls, though an enticing brightness about the eyes compensated. "Mary Sutter, the midwife?" he asked.

"Yes, I am Mary Sutter." The young woman looked from the address she had inscribed that afternoon in her small, leather-bound notebook to the harried man in front of her, wondering how he could possibly know who she was. He was all angles, and his sharp chin gave the impression of discipline, though his uncombed hair and unbuttoned vest were damp with sweat.

"Oh, thank God," he said, and, catching her by the elbow, pulled her inside and slammed the door shut on the cold April rain and the stray warble of a bugle in the distance. James Blevens knew Mary Sutter only by reputation. *She is good, even better than her mother*, people said. Now he formed an indelible impression of attractiveness, though there was nothing attractive about her. Her features were far too coarse, her hair far too wild and already beginning to silver. People said she was young, but you could not tell that by looking at her. She was an odd one, this Mary Sutter.

A kerosene lantern flickered in the late afternoon dimness, revealing shelves of medical instruments: scales, tensile prongs, hinged forceps, monaural and chest stethoscopes, jars of pickled fetal pigs, ether stoppered in azure glass, a femur bone stripped in acid, a human skull, a stomach floating in brine, jars of medicines, an apothecary's mortar and pestle. Mary could barely tear her eyes from the bounty.

"She is here, at last," the man said over his shoulder.

Mary Sutter peered into the darkness and saw a young woman lying on an exam table, a blanket thrown across her swollen belly, betraying the unmistakable exhaustion of late labor.

"Excuse me, but were you expecting me?" Mary asked.

"Yes, yes," he said, waving her question away with irritation. "Didn't my boy send you here?"

"No. I came to see you on my own. Are you Dr. Blevens?"

"Of course I am."

Now that the time had come, Mary felt almost shy, the humiliation of her afternoon rearing up, along with the anger that had propelled her here, looking for a last chance. On her way, she had waded through crowds, barely conscious of a mounting commotion, lifting her skirts out of the mud, struggling past the tannery and the livery, finally arriving at the two-story frame building with its unpainted door and narrow, steep stairs, so unlike the echoing marble hallways where she had just been refused entry. And all the while, newspaper boys had been yelling *Extra!* and tributaries of people had been trickling toward the Capitol, and still she had pressed on.

"Dr. Blevens, I came here today—" Mary stopped and exhaled. All the hope of the past year spilled over as she stumbled over her words. "Today I sat in the lobby of the medical college for four hours waiting for Dr. Marsh, and he didn't even have the courtesy to see me." Mary shut out the memory of her afternoon spent in the unwelcoming misery of the Albany Medical College, where after several hours the corpulent clerk had finally hissed, *Dr. Marsh no longer wishes to receive letters of application from you, so you are to respectfully desist in any further petition.*

"When he refused to see me, I decided to come and ask something of you," Mary said.

"Would you mind asking me later?" Blevens asked, propelling Mary toward the young woman. "I need your help. This is Bonnie Miles. Her husband dropped her here early this afternoon. He said she has lost a child before—her first. I think the baby's head is stuck."

Mary pulled off her gloves and unwrapped her shawl, her quest forgotten for the moment, all her attention focused on the woman's exhaustion and youth. Bonnie was small-boned, tiny in all her features, too young, Mary thought, perhaps fifteen, maybe seventeen. Her hips were too narrow, which might be the problem Dr. Blevens had encountered.

"Have you been laboring long?" Mary asked.

The doctor answered for her, speaking quickly and nervously. "She cannot say. Since the night, at least."

Mary lifted her gaze from the girl to appraise the doctor with a cool, steady glance. "No chloroform, no forceps?"

"Why do you think I called you? I've seen enough of the damage those can do. I'm a surgeon, for God's sake, not a butcher. Please," the doctor said, "I need your help." Of late, surgeons had entered the obstetrics trade, but there had been too many mistakes to make him feel comfortable. He didn't like administering chloroform to ease the mother's pain, because babies ended up languishing in the womb, and doctors had to go hunting for them with forceps. Too many women had bled, too many babies' skulls had been crushed. He would stick with the ailments of men: hatchet blows and factory burns.

"You'll help me?" the girl asked.

As Mary smoothed the blanket, she thought that the girl resembled Jenny, though she lacked Jenny's distinguishing clarity of skin. But the wide-set eyes, the high cheekbones, and the bright lips had emerged from the same well of beauty as Mary's twin. Once, when Mary was very young, she had asked her mother what "twin" meant, and her mother, who had understood the root of the question, had answered, *God does not give out his gifts equally, even to those who have shared a womb.*

"My last one died," Bonnie said, whispering, drawing Mary close to her, her face transforming from a feverish daze to one of grief.

"I beg your pardon?"

"The baby before this," Bonnie said, her eyes half closed. "I didn't know it was labor I was taken with, you see?"

The ignorance! It was *exactly* like Jenny. But Jenny's ignorance was something altogether different, a refusal to engage, to exert herself. A lack of curiosity.

Outside, above the street clatter of carriages and vendors came the hard clang of the fire bell, and cries of "On to the South!"

Blevens rushed to the window and threw it open as Mary whispered to Bonnie not to worry. The rising strains of a band joined the bugle, producing a festive, off-tune march that beckoned like a piper. A swelling crowd hurried along the turnpike, shoulders and wool hats bent against the rain. In the distance the flat pop of gunfire sounded.

"You there! Hello? Can you give me the news?" Blevens cried.

A man who had stopped to don an oilskin looked up, revealing a slick, battered face, pocked, the doctor was certain, at the ironworks where the spitting metal often scarred workers' faces.

"Haven't you heard?" the man shouted. "The Carolinians fired on Fort Sumter!"

"Has Lincoln called for men?" the doctor asked, but the scarred man melted into the stream of revelers pushing down the muddy turnpike toward the music as if something were reeling them in. James Blevens slammed down the window and turned.

"I cannot believe it," he said. "It is war."

Bonnie seized Mary's wrist, and Mary said, "Do you want to scare her?"

"Sorry," Blevens said, but he was agitated, glancing again toward the window.

"I'll need scissors, lard, and any rags you have," Mary said. "And water."

With a last look over his shoulder, Blevens scurried to assemble the requested supplies. Bonnie nodded off into the deep sleep that overcame women between contractions. Mary probed her belly, feeling for the baby's spine. Often it was the baby's position in the womb that caused delay. There were also other reasons, worse reasons, that Mary did not yet want to entertain. Look first, her mother always said, for the common.

Bonnie was thin—undernourished even—but even through that thin wall of belly, Mary could not detect the rope of spine she was looking for.

"Bonnie."

The girl snapped from her deep sleep and fixed her gaze on Mary.

"I have to put my hand inside you. Do you understand? I have to confirm where the baby's head is."

The girl nodded, but Mary knew that she did not understand. "You keep looking at me, do you understand? Don't close your eyes."

Mary slipped her hand into the warm glove of Bonnie's body and began to probe the baby's head for the telltale V, where the suture lines of the scalp met in ridges at the back. Bonnie's water had not yet burst and Mary worked gingerly, pressing gently against the bulging sac around the baby's head, taking care not to snag the membrane. Yes, there was the V. She ran her hand along the lines, keeping Bonnie's gaze locked on hers, smiling encouragement as she searched for the obstacle.

"Bonnie," Mary said gently, withdrawing her hand, wiping it on a rag. "Your baby is coming out face up. That's why you're having so much trouble. I have to turn the baby. It will make things easier for both of you. It's going to be uncomfortable, but I'll do it quickly."

Mary nodded to Dr. Blevens; at her summons, he strode across the room and took Bonnie's hands in his. Mary slipped again inside Bonnie and slowly fitted her fingers around the baby's skull. With her other hand, she felt through the abdominal wall for the baby's arms and legs. She established a grip. She was standing now, her right hand deep inside Bonnie, the other on her belly. The wave of contraction hit hard. Bonnie's mouth moved, but no sound came out. Dr. Blevens was leaning forward, his face inches from Bonnie's, whispering encouragement into her ear. When the contraction relaxed, Mary grasped the baby's skull and made a percussive shove with her left hand, rolling the baby in a wave. Bonnie writhed under the abuse, arching her back off the table, then falling again. Through the tidal swell of the next two contractions, Mary held the child in place, keeping the baby locked in its new position, the muscled womb clamping down on her fingertips. From outside, Mary could hear more shouts, but even these could not distract her now. All her movements, decisions, and thoughts came from a well deep inside her. When she was certain that the baby would not roll back, she carefully withdrew her hands, and the rest of the delivery proceeded. Mary looked only at Bonnie, thought only of Bonnie and the baby. She was authoritative when Bonnie faltered, stern when she panicked, and unflagging when, screaming, Bonnie expelled a boy in a rush of amniotic fluid. Mary wiped the small flag of his gender along with the rest of him, and then swaddled him in a blanket that the doctor handed her. There was no deformation. The child was perfect, if small. She judged this one at nine months' gestation, but maybe less.

"Extraordinary. I was certain the head was too large," Blevens said.

"It's a common enough mistake."

Efficient but tender, Mary went about her work with a kind of informality. She tucked the mewling infant into Bonnie's grateful arms and tied off the cord after the afterbirth slithered out. There was little blood. The girl had not even torn.

"It's the lard," Mary said, wiping her soaked skirts with a towel. "Massage it into the flesh beforehand, a bit at a time."

Blevens tucked in the ends of the blanket that had fallen away, but he knew it to be an insignificant contribution, the act of a maiden aunt after the danger had passed.

"Do allow me to pay you," he said, but Mary dismissed this offer with a wave of her hand.

"Where is her husband?" Mary asked.

"I don't know. He ran in with her and then left." Blevens looked around the room as if the boy might suddenly appear.

"But where will she go?"

Blevens shrugged. His rooms were not made for keeping patients overnight.

"If you like, I can take her home with me. My mother and I have a lying-in room. She can stay with us until she's recovered."

He protested, and Mary shook it off as if it were nothing, but James Blevens knew it wasn't nothing. The girl and her husband were poor farmers. James had surmised that much when the boy had dropped Bonnie off. They would never be able to pay for any care, not even room and board. Her offer was very generous, more generous than James had any right to expect given that she had been called in at the last minute. But now he recalled the earlier confusion.

"Miss Sutter, what was it you wanted from me this afternoon?"

Mary wiped her hands on her ruined skirts. Her birthing apron was at home, along with the rest of her medicine, rubber sheets, scissors, and rags. "You have already seen me turn a child. I am just as skilled with a previa, or twins. But I want more. I want to study. I want to know more about anatomy, physiology. The *something* I cannot see." It was the speech she had meant for Dr. Marsh. She began to speak in a rush, the words tumbling out. "For instance, the problem of why some women seize in labor. I know that headaches and light sensitivity precede it, but do they trigger it? Is it like other seizure disorders? I know that sometimes it's caused by a rapid revolution of blood to the head, or a too severely felt labor, but why? I was reading in *The Process of Parturition*—"

Dr. Blevens swiveled to look at his bookshelf and then turned back to her. "Aren't deliveries enough for you?"

Mary's gaze was covetous. "I want to understand *everything*," she said. "Isn't it all connected? Isn't the body a system? How can I understand a part if I do not understand the whole?"

Mary recognized Blevens's look: the tilting of the head, the gaze of incredulity. Why was she always such a surprise to people? In her childhood her father had often greeted her questions—Is the Hudson's tidal nature a detriment or a help to transportation? What is the height of the world's largest mountain? What is the true nature of the earth's center?—with exhalations of astonishment.

"Miss Sutter, what precisely do you want?"

"I want to become a doctor. The Albany Medical College won't admit me. I want you to teach me."

"I beg your pardon?"

"Many fine doctors have only apprenticed—"

"Miss Sutter—"

"Consider what you just saw, what I just did for you. I work hard. You would not be disappointed. And I could teach you midwifery!" *This is it*, Mary thought. *I have to convince this man.*

Blevens could understand the young woman's enthusiasm for medicine, and he wondered now what William Stipp would make of her. She was nearly as windblown and desperate as Blevens had been a decade ago, when he had accosted Stipp much the way Miss Sutter was accosting him now.

Blevens sighed and said, "I am terribly sorry, but what you propose is impossible."

"It is not impossible."

"It is. I'm going to enlist. They'll need surgeons."

"But you don't know what will happen. You don't know. Maybe this is the end, maybe it's all over—"

"Have you gone mad? The war has just started!"

The baby began to cry and James Blevens cursed. They had been whispering, trying not to disturb Bonnie.

Blevens said, "I am most grateful to you today for your help, and I will pay you, but I cannot—"

"But you *can*," Mary said. "Dr. Blevens, if you take me on—"

He heaved a sigh. "Miss Sutter, even if there were no war, and we were to do this, you would have no lectures. No dissecting lab. You would see no surgeries except the sporadic ones I perform here. And then when I finished teaching you, you would have no credential—"

"Please," she said. "Please. It is all I want."

The kerosene lantern threw shadows across the walls and floor. In the flickering light, Mary Sutter and James Blevens stood as opposed now as they had been united moments before. Only the soft whimpering of the baby broke the silence. James Blevens could feel the strength of the woman's desire. They echoed memories of his own beginnings, his own desperate pleas when he was starting, when getting into a medical college had seemed an impossible goal.

"I'm sorry. I cannot," Dr. Blevens said.

"I see." Even as Mary spoke, she modulated her tone, but it was no use. Yearning and heartbreak combined with fatigue, and even as she turned her attention to Bonnie, dutiful as always, remembering to check Bonnie's belly to make certain the uterus was still contracting, she said, "It would be nothing to you to teach me. Nothing."

"Are you always this persistent?"

"Always," Mary said.

"Miss Sutter, you helped me a great deal today. I am grateful. No doubt Bonnie is grateful. You demonstrated great skill. Remarkable skill. But I cannot help you to become a physician. What you are asking is impossible."

"Well, then," Mary said, nodding, remonstrating with herself not to say *Thank you for your time*, or other like idiocies. *Do not cede,* she thought. *Keep your spine straight.* "You'll have to help me to get Bonnie home. I haven't a carriage."

James Blevens took in the disappointment of the woman who had helped him and felt, not for the first time, that he was hopeless with women. He didn't understand them. His wife, Sarah, living in Manhattan City, would agree. He should be given credit for asking for help from a midwife; no other doctor in Albany would have capitulated control, but Sarah, if she ever heard of this, would only say that he had failed yet again.

"My carriage is in the back. I'll bring it around front," he said.

Blevens tacked a note to his door for the delinquent husband and then went back inside to retrieve Bonnie. Mary followed behind with the child, swaddled against the rain. He had already padded the bed of the open carriage with horse blankets for Bonnie, and as he laid her inside, Mary noticed how tender he was with her, as if he knew what it was to be a woman.

The nearby slaughterhouse smokers were snuffed for the night, but the air felt compressed and humid in the tapering rain. From the direction of State Street, a gaseous yellow haze hovered, a drumbeat speeding the distance from the revelry to their carriage, the brass notes lagging behind. As the horse plodded through the streets, James Blevens and Mary Sutter did not speak. Witnesses to intimacy, they could find nothing now to say except for directions given and clarified. It was awkward to have spoken of desire, revelation, disappointment. Only a mile separated Dove Street from Dr. Blevens's surgery, but the drive felt like a hundred.

The Sutter home was one of the new kinds of row houses made from quarried stone: deep, rather than wide, windows aligned singly one atop the other in three neat stories, an iron railing ascending the steep stairs from the sidewalk of slate. Dr. Blevens tied the horses and carried Bonnie in his arms; Mary cradled the infant and glided up the stairs behind him, letting the maid answer the bell. Inside, an open stairway soared to the next floor and a third beyond. A newel post stood sentry, and balusters supported a carved walnut balustrade. Off the hallway, French doors opened into a parlor; on a small table, tulips bloomed in a glass vase.

Blevens had not expected wealth.

"Is my mother home?" Mary asked, unwrapping her shawl with one arm while managing the baby with the other.

"Out, Miss, on a call." The maid calmly surveyed the pair of guests. "Shall I set the table for two more?"

"A tray, please, upstairs for the new mother," Mary said, and climbed the stairs with Blevens following. Sconces burned tapered candles; on the stairs, brass rods held back a cascading maroon runner. Mary settled Bonnie under a thick comforter in a wide bed in a room at the top of the stairs while Dr. Blevens waited in the hallway outside. A walnut bookshelf lined the long hall, which was open to the stairwell. The shelves held a medical library to envy: *Gray's Anatomy, A Pharmocologia,* and the aforementioned *The Process of Parturition.* Blevens was holding the text open when Mary emerged some ten minutes later.

"Wellon's Bookstore," Mary said. "He gets me anything I ask for."

"You have read all of these?"

"Of course." She excused herself and disappeared into a bedroom. When she emerged she had changed her clothes. She wore a clean, high-necked dress of no distinguishing feature. It was as if she cared nothing for beauty, though it was clear that someone in the home did.

Blevens trailed Mary down the stairs. "Do you often take ladies for lying-in?"

"Rarely. And only if they are destitute."

In the entry, Mary retrieved Blevens's hat from the stand and held it out for him as she opened the door. There would be no dinner for him at the Sutter home tonight, no matter what the maid had offered. Outside, rain was drumming on the red leather benches of his carriage, the cobbles, the stone stoop, the houses opposite.

"Good night, Dr. Blevens."

"You must understand, Miss Sutter," Blevens said, "that I am not in a position to help you." The excuse sounded lamentable. *I am not in a position.* "Surely, with your resources—" He made a vague gesture toward an elegant crystal vase, as if its presence on a burnished walnut table in her foyer could somehow persuade Dr. Marsh to admit her to the college.

"One cannot buy what one truly wants, Dr. Blevens. Haven't you learned that yet?"

Blevens pulled his coin purse from his pocket. "I insist on paying you."

"You cannot buy *me*, either."

"I meant only to thank you."

"Good-bye."

Blevens sighed, replaced his coin purse, put on his hat, and murmured a good-bye. He would have liked to have helped her, would have, too, if he could. But the war. Even now, he was thinking of following the noise of the band still playing in the distance despite the rain, which had become a torrent, wind gusting through the door. He was about to step over the threshold when an open carriage pulled up and two women and a male companion tumbled out, wrapped in horse blankets. A clap of thunder hurried them up the stairs and into the foyer, the women brushing water from the puffed shoulders of their coats and shaking sodden umbrellas. The blankets were soaked through and the women laughed as they unwound themselves and began unpinning wet hats more stylish than the one Mary Sutter still wore perched atop her wild curls. (Blevens thought, *She doesn't care for herself; she neglects even the simplest rituals of dress.*) It was obvious that these two were related in some way, even though there were only hints of resemblance—the same long nose, large eyes, and square chin as Mary, but they were more accurately and pleasingly executed, especially on the younger of the two women, though the older was youngish and alive, with luminescent skin and curls tamer than Mary's.

"A friend of yours, Mary?" The older woman smiled and extended a gloved hand, but, noticing its waterlogged state, laughingly peeled off the glove and then extended her hand again. "I am Amelia Sutter, Mary's mother." If she was surprised to see a strange man in her hallway with her daughter, she did not show it. If anything, she seemed delighted. "How do you do?"

"James Blevens. I am quite well, thanks to your daughter. She saved me. She took over in the middle of a difficult birth and has also taken in the mother and child. I was just about to leave."

Mary became furious, suddenly, at his courtly tone, as if they hadn't been arguing moments before.

Amelia glanced at Mary and then back to Blevens. "Do you teach at the medical college?"

"No, Miss Sutter came upon me when a young woman in labor arrived unexpectedly at my surgery."

Amelia looked inquiringly at Mary, but Mary shook her head. An understanding passed between them, and a fleeting look of pity altered Amelia's features. Mary shrugged her shoulders and the moment passed, but James Blevens knew that the mother had known of Mary's appointment.

"Well," Amelia said. She looked outside, where James Blevens's carriage was thoroughly soaked and his horse shivering in the rain. "Oh dear. This is impossible. You cannot leave now. The weather is beastly. You'll be drenched. And we've just come from the rally. There is no one left, not even the vagrants. Just the band, sheltered under the Capitol's portico. And all the rosters that everyone signed to enlist are wetted to shreds. So you see it's no good. You must stay to supper."

She pulled off her coat, revealing a mourning dress of deep black. Her pleasant affect was in such contrast to the attire that Blevens wondered if she merely liked the color.

"That is very kind of you, but I cannot impose."

"He was just leaving, Mother," Mary said. "It would be rude to keep him."

"Yes, I—" Blevens gestured at the rain.

"But this won't do at all. Jenny, would you please—" Amelia turned and, seeing her other daughter waiting patiently, said, "Do forgive me. May I present my daughter, Jenny? She is Mary's twin. And our neighbor, Thomas Fall." She rested a hand on the shoulders of the two young people beside her. "My son Christian is lagging behind; he could barely part with all the excitement even though he'll be drowned. He'll have to join us in progress, I'm afraid." Amelia patted Jenny's shoulder and said, "Jenny, darling, please ask the maid to send her son to take the doctor's horse to the carriage house. He'll need to be dried down and hayed."

Jenny dutifully went to deliver the message before Blevens could refuse. There was no gracious way to decline the invitation that Mary had so blatantly withheld. But he did not want to stay. His presence would only goad. He thought longingly of the solitude of his rented rooms on State Street and pictured Mary Sutter scolding her family after he left for their guileless welcome. He had withheld the favor she perceived he could easily give, and there was no way to make that right.

Amelia turned her attention to Mary. "A delivery, you said? Is she all right? Did things go well? Do you have any questions?" On Amelia's river of words, everyone was swept down the hallway to the dining room, where a fire blazed in an expansive hearth and maids had already expanded the table to set more places. There were six settings around the linen-covered table. Mary took her place, with her back to the fire, and did not look at Blevens. Jenny and Amelia exchanged glances, trying to discern from Mary's stony silence how her day at the medical college had ended with a guest for dinner whom she was ignoring. Thomas Fall, the only one unaware, it seemed, of the day's expected role in Mary's future, was pulling out his chair and speaking eagerly of the rally and Lincoln's call for men.

It was a subject that Blevens was impatient to discuss.

But it was difficult to discuss anything. There was something unformed about Thomas Fall, Blevens thought as the young man began to talk. His conversation left little room for interruption, though the young man spoke with the confidence of one who had been accepted and encouraged at this table before. Idealistic, ambitious, Fall spoke about the war with intelligence and naiveté both: "Lincoln wants seventy-five thousand for the immediate protection of Washington City," he began. The *Argus*, it turned out, had published a special edition with Lincoln's plea. Virginia threatened to the south; the Rebels could be upon the city at any moment. If they captured Washington, the war would be over. A coup. Slavery forever. Fall was certain that the Rebels would soon be defeated, which Blevens also believed, for the North had the advantage in manufacturing and railroads, but it was the flicker of excitability, the flare of eagerness that showed when Fall babbled on about the glory of battle that betrayed his youth, though his clothes were better cut than Blevens's, attesting to greater wealth.

As he spoke, it turned out that Fall's confidence was well founded: all three women yielded the conversation to him, and not solely for reasons of hospitality. The younger sister, Jenny, was adoring. But Mary attended perhaps more intensely, albeit covertly. Glances of sharp admiration, a softening of her features. Moments when she ceased eating to gaze, then remembered herself and passed the salt or the butter, though no one had asked. When Fall finally solicited Blevens's opinions, Mary became inattentive as he probed the possibility of greater bloodshed than Fall expected, but he did not want to be rude or alarm the women, and so he droned on about the necessity of controlling the railroads, which sounded boring even to him.

Christian Sutter, the brother, arrived during the meat course. He was tall, curly-headed, a mop of hair, a grin, all confidence, younger than his two sisters. Charm had won him everything in life, it seemed, including his mother's adoration. He took the foot of the table. No father had been mentioned. Their mourning must not have been recent, Blevens decided. This was a family adjusted to whatever losses it had sustained. Happily settled at his place, Christian beamed and said, "Did you know that they've already formed a regiment? The 25th. It's a good number, don't you think?"

Amelia Sutter threw her son a fearful, longing glance. Pride muzzled instinct, though it was a battle. A sudden smile turned tremulous, then disappeared altogether as Thomas and Christian agreed that immediate enlistment was required of any self-respecting Northerner.

For her part, Mary had shaped a more formed opinion of Blevens during the soup course than she had been able to do in his surgery rooms. Seated opposite, he comported himself with the manners of a man not unaccustomed to either money or talk. The dishevelment of his surgery rooms did not coincide with this new picture.

Thomas and Christian were arguing about Texas. "If there is to be any fight at all in Texas, it will have to be soon, because they've just emptied the forts of Federal soldiers—"

"Dr. Blevens is going to the war, too," Mary said, interrupting.

It was as if someone had declared war in the dining room. Blevens hurriedly said, "Yes, as a surgeon. One doesn't wish for bloodshed, but—"

"But you do, don't you, Dr. Blevens?" Mary said. "You want to see what can happen to the human body. You want to see inside it. You want to solve its mysteries." She had sharpened her voice and set down her heavy silver knife. The roast was delicious, but unimportant. "Not that you should be ashamed. It is no less than I would wish to do. Given the opportunity."

"Mary," Amelia said.

"It is not shameful to press one's point, Mother." She turned again to the doctor. "I haven't misspoken your aspirations in going to the war, have I, Dr. Blevens?"

Mary Sutter was calling in his debt. He was to be made to apologize in front of everyone. "Miss Sutter, I am very sorry that I cannot help you. But with your gift for persistence, I doubt very much you will not someday claim your opportunity."

"Help you how, Mary?" Amelia asked.

Mary ignored her. "But I will only be able to claim it if I am offered it. Tell me, Dr. Blevens, in your opinion, is there a limit to how much knowledge one person is allowed to accumulate? Have I reached my quota?"

Blevens thought again of his rooms on State Street. He could be beside his own fire right now, looking through his microscope. "Miss Sutter, you have my deepest respect and gratitude. But I cannot help you."

"Dr. Blevens, do you know of the woman Miss Nightingale?" Mary asked.

"Do I seem as illiterate as all that?"

"Have you read her *Notes on Nursing*?"

"Yes, as a matter of fact, I have."

Mary registered surprise, but forged on. "One of the reasons my mother and I are the best midwives in Albany is that we read the latest medical literature."

"You speak, Mary, as if our accomplishments were daggers," Amelia said.

Mary Sutter laid her hands in her lap and rearranged her expression into one of tolerant hospitality, but behind the benign visage sparkled the same intense determination she had shown in Blevens's rooms that afternoon. She fixed him with a stare.

"Are you aware, Dr. Blevens, that in the last year, Miss Nightingale has refused to leave her room?" Mary asked.

"I beg your pardon?"

"Miss Nightingale, brilliant lecturer, member of the Royal Statistical Society, the woman who saved the British army in the Crimea, has shut herself in a hotel room in London and refuses to leave it. I am not saying that she is mad. Apparently, she is quite coherent. But averse to society for some unrevealed reason."

"It is possible the war both made and unmade Miss Nightingale. The deprivation, the difficulty—"

"That's possible, but I believe Miss Nightingale has hidden herself away from society in order to be heard. I think she knows that people would not listen quite so intently to her if she were always parading her achievements in front of everyone. I myself think that no woman should have to hide." A pause. "Or perhaps Miss Nightingale *is* mad. It's interesting that no one really knows."

Glasses clinked and throats cleared. Jenny wiped her lips with her napkin. The halting silence around the table was characterized not by shame, but by a vague weariness. Mary unfurled was formidable and her family all knew it and, it seemed, sometimes despaired of it.

"I do beg your pardon, but are you suggesting that my refusal to help you will somehow render you mad?" Blevens said.

"I fail to see how comparing female intelligence to madness is going to help your case, Mary," Thomas Fall said, emerging from the hush to jolly along his future sister-in-law.

James Blevens raised his hands in concession. "You did not want me at your table tonight, Miss Sutter. You have had to endure my company after I disappointed you."

"How? How did he disappoint you?" Amelia asked, but Thomas Fall stepped in once again.

"Our Mary is not quite as inhospitable as she seems." Thomas threw Mary a gentle smile, which she returned with a flicker of her own. "If you wish to receive a pass from Mary, you need only be a woman in the last throes of childbirth. She likes the needy best, I think."

"Yes, she was remarkable today," Blevens said. "As I suspect she usually is."

His compliment earned him no correspondent smile from Mary, who took a sip of wine and looked away. Amelia reached her hand to Mary, but Mary shook her head.

Taking charge of the table, Thomas abruptly changed the subject, accustomed, it seemed, to navigating the family's more difficult shores. "Dr. Blevens, before we all go off, I'd be happy to take you out to Ireland's Corners. I keep orchards on the Loudon Road. Apples and cherries. I have hopes that the New York Railroad will one day extend a line northward. Think of the prospects of fruit picked in the morning being delivered to Manhattan City by evening of the same day."

"Is this a family business?" Blevens asked. He reached for a glass of water, giving sidelong glances to his dinner companions, all of whom suddenly held Thomas Fall in a sympathetic gaze.

Thomas set down his fork. "It was, yes. But last October my father and mother died in a carriage accident. Hit by a runaway."

"I beg your pardon. I didn't mean to—"

"No. Your question was welcome."

Jenny reached out her hand and enfolded his hand in hers.

"I do beg your pardon," James said. "That is very recent."

"We had just moved into town. Father was not used to the traffic."

"I am sorry." Blevens wished now that Bonnie Miles had never walked through the doors of his surgery this afternoon. Nothing had gone well from that moment. Upstairs, he could hear the baby crying, and footsteps climbing the stairs. A maid, going to Bonnie's aid. He cast around for something to say. "If you don't mind my asking a practical question, but with no one to give your business to, how will you enlist?"

Amelia said to Thomas, "If Mr. Sutter were still with us, he would have gladly taken control of the orchards until your return. And have built you a rail line."

Of course, Blevens thought. Why hadn't he registered this before? This was the family of Nathaniel Sutter, of the New York Railroad. This explained the beautiful home and furnishings far better than did the income of two midwives. He tried to remember exactly when Sutter had died. Less than a year ago also? Their mourning had been brief, but perhaps they had found solace in one another.

"Nathaniel would have built you two rail lines," Amelia said, extending an arm across the pale linen to the beautiful daughter. The quiet one, too, it seemed, for she hadn't yet spoken a word, though Jenny appeared unruffled by her own silence. She had the prize, the boy next door, and therefore did not covet the spotlight for herself.

"I have an excellent overseer," Thomas said, "who knows the business far better than I do. I rely on him."

Cake was being served, coffee poured. A few more minutes, fifteen at the most, and then James could beg fatigue. He wondered now whether Amelia regretted her hospitality as much as her daughter Mary did. So far, he had insulted Mary twice, revived grief in all of them, and invaded a family dinner on the brink of a war. It seemed there was no way he could redeem himself. He was picturing the Sutters' conversation after he left—*Mary, how did you ever bring such an odd man home?*—when a maid flung open the door.

"She's bleeding, ma'am."

A flash of skirts and Mary was out of the room, Blevens racing after her up the stairs two at a time.

In the lying-in room, Bonnie's bedclothes were saturated with blood, the baby stowed safely on a pillow by the maid. Bonnie's eyes were saucers of astonishment.

"I felt something warm," she said.

"A tear," Mary said, thinking of her hands deep inside Bonnie earlier that day.

But Dr. Blevens was already raising Bonnie's reddened nightgown while shielding her nakedness with a blanket. "Lie back; don't be afraid." Swiftly, he palpated the pillow of her abdomen, and after a few minutes began a circular massage. Behind him, Mary Sutter stood reluctantly impressed. He had been hunting for the uterus, to see if it had relaxed, which obviously it had, because as soon as the massage began, the flood had stopped. The massage contracted the uterus, shutting off the open blood vessels where the placenta had been attached. This was the first step in any maternal hemorrhage.

The tide abated, Blevens took Bonnie's hand and pressed her fingers deep into her stomach.

"Do you feel that?" he asked, helping Bonnie find the hard ball of her uterus underneath her navel.

"What is that?" she cried.

"Your womb," Blevens said, smiling now. "Yours is a bit recalcitrant for some reason. You'll need to rub it every few minutes so that it will keep contracting and you won't bleed. Can you do that?" Over his shoulder, he called to Mary, "Have you any ergot?"

Reduced to the role of nurse in her own lying-in room, Mary dispensed the medicine and then called the maids to help her change the bedding. While everything was made right, Dr. Blevens scooped up the baby and retreated to the window, where he bounced the child in his arms. Then Mary led Blevens to the kitchen so he could wash his hands. His frock coat was edged in blood.

Mary said, "You know far more than you let on this afternoon, Dr. Blevens. Did you even need my help in the delivery?"

The maids scurried out, pretending not to pay attention. Later, this conversation would be told in the kitchens on Arbor Hill in the Sixth Ward: *And then the doctor said. And then the Miss said.* Outside, the pigs would be rooting in the garbage and the maids would be saying to their husbands, "And her so haughty."

Blevens said, "I don't practice enough to feel successful in deliveries, but I am not completely ignorant of the needs of women. Bonnie's hemorrhage was easily controlled, merely atony of the uterus. You would have done the same."

She could barely contain her humiliation. She would not have done the same, and the failure of her usual unerring intuition made her furious. She would have hunted for the tear, wasting precious time. "Why do you think I knocked at your door today, Dr. Blevens? Did you really think that I would prefer to apprentice when I could attend a college? Did you really think I wasn't at the end of my choices?" She was pinning and unpinning her hair, the curls disobedient, refusing to be locked in place.

Laughter echoed from the upstairs, where Amelia had gone to supervise, having already taken graceful leave of Blevens in the hallway. Jenny and Thomas were closeted away in the parlor, lovers with shortened time. Christian had gone out again after shaking Blevens's hand.

"I'll say good night," Blevens said, bowing.

The front door swung shut behind him, sounding like the end of something. Outside, the rain had not let up, and he remembered too late that his horse and carriage had been quartered in the carriage house in the alley behind. He should have exited from the kitchen, where the door led to the yard and alleyway. For a moment, he paused on the stoop, but then hunched his shoulders and walked down the windswept, rainy block, turned right, and turned again into the alley, where he located the Sutter carriage house and led his horse and carriage from the warm confines into the dreary night.

from

My Name Is Memory

by

Ann Brashares

The latest novel from the *New York Times* bestselling author.

Daniel has spent centuries falling in love with the same girl. Life after life, he and Sophia (despite her changing name and form) have been drawn together and torn apart—and he remembers it all. But just when Sophia finally awakens to their shared past, the mysterious force that has always separated them reappears. Ultimately, they must come to understand what stands in the way of their love if they are ever to spend a lifetime together.

"An inventive, romantic, highly pleasurable ride through time." —The Washington Post

I HAVE LIVED more than a thousand years. I have died countless times. I forget precisely how many times. My memory is an extraordinary thing, but it is not perfect. I am human.

The early lives blur a bit. The arc of your soul follows the pattern of each of your lives. It is macrocosmic. There was my childhood. There have been many childhoods. And even in the early part of my soul I reached adulthood many times. These days, in every one of my infancies, the memory comes faster. We go through the motions. We look oddly at the world around us. We remember.

I say "we" and I mean myself, my soul, my selves, my many lives. I say "we" and I also mean the other ones like me who have the Memory, the conscious record of experience on this earth that survives every death. There aren't many, I know. Maybe one in a century, one born out of millions. We find one another rarely, but believe me, there are others. At least one of them has a memory far more extraordinary than mine.

I have been born and died many times in many places. The space between them is the same. I wasn't in Bethlehem for Christ's birth. I never saw the glory that was Rome. I never bowed to Charlemagne. At that time I was scratching out a crop in Anatolia, speaking a dialect unintelligible to the villages north and south. Only God and the devil can be counted on for all the thrilling parts.

The great hits of history go along without the notice of most. I read about them in books like everybody else.

Sometimes I feel more akin to houses and trees than to my fellow human beings. I stand around watching the waves of people come and go. Their lives are short, but mine is long. Sometimes I imagine myself as a post driven into the ocean's edge.

I've never had a child, and I've never gotten old. I don't know why. I have seen beauty in countless things. I have fallen in love, and she is the one who endures. I killed her once and died for her many times and I still have nothing to show for it. I always search for her; I always remember her. I carry the hope that someday she will remember me.

SHE HADN'T KNOWN him very long. He'd shown up there at the beginning of eleventh grade. It was a small town and a small school district. You kept seeing the same kids year after year. He was a junior when he came, the same as her, but he seemed older somehow.

She'd heard many things about where and how he had spent the previous seventeen years of his life, but she doubted any of them were true. He was in a mental institution before he came to Hopewood, people said. His father was in jail and he lived by himself. His mother was killed, they said, most likely by his father. He always wore long sleeves, somebody said, because he had burns on his arms. He'd never defended himself against these stories, as far as she knew, and never offered any alternatives.

And though Lucy didn't believe the rumors, she understood the thing they were getting at. Daniel was different, even as he tried not to be. His face was proud, but there was a feeling of tragedy about him. It seemed to her as though no one had taken care of him and he didn't even realize it. One time she saw him standing in the cafeteria by the window while everyone else was jostling past him with their clattering trays, yakking a mile a minute, and he just looked completely lost. There was something about the way he looked at that moment that made her think he was the loneliest person in the world.

When he first appeared at school there was a lot of commotion about him because he was extremely good-looking. He was tall and strong-boned and self-possessed, and his clothes were a little nicer than most other kids'. At first the coaches were sniffing around for him to play football because of his size, but he didn't pursue it. As it was a small town and a bored town and a hopeful town, kids talked and rumors started. The rumors were ennobling at first, but then he made some mistakes. He didn't show up at Melody Sanderson's Halloween party, even though she invited him personally in the hallway, and everybody saw it. He talked to Sonia Frye straight through the annual junior/senior picnic, even though she was an untouchable freak to people like Melody. It was a delicate social ecosystem they lived in, and most people got scared off him by the first winter.

Except Lucy. She herself didn't know why not. She didn't respect Melody or her posse of yeah-girls, but she trod carefully. She had marks against her to begin with, and she didn't want to be an outcast. She couldn't do that to her mother, not after what she'd already been through with her sister. Nor was Lucy the kind who liked difficult boys. She didn't.

She had the weird idea—kind of a fantasy, actually—that she could help him. She knew what it was like on the outside and the inside at this school, and she knew what it took to maintain yourself through both. She sensed that he bore a heavier weight than most other people, and it gave her a strange, aching empathy for him. She honored herself with the idea that maybe he needed her, that maybe she was the one who could understand him.

He showed no sign of sharing this view. In almost two years he hadn't spoken to her once. Well, one time she'd stepped on his shoelace and apologized to him and he'd stared at her and muttered something. She'd felt nagging and uneasy afterward, and her mind kept going back to it, trying to figure out what he'd said and what he'd meant, but she finally decided that she hadn't done anything wrong and it was his problem going around with his shoe untied in the senior hallway at three in the afternoon.

"Do you think I'm overthinking this?" she'd asked Marnie.

Marnie looked at her as though it took restraint not to claw at her hair. "Yes, I do. I think you are overthinking this. If there was a movie about you it would be called *I Am Overthinking This.*"

She'd laughed at the time and worried later. Marnie wasn't trying to be mean. Marnie loved her better and more honestly than anyone else in the world, with the possible exception of her mother, who loved her intensely if not honestly. Marnie hated to see her spend so much of herself on someone who didn't care.

Lucy suspected he was some kind of genius. Not that he did or said anything to let you know. But once she'd sat beside him in English class, sneaking looks when the class was discussing Shakespeare. She'd seen him, his big shoulders huddled over his notebook, writing sonnets from memory, one after the other, in beautiful slanting script that made her think of Thomas Jefferson drafting the Declaration of Independence. He had a look on his face that made her believe he was as far as he could be from the small, boxy classroom with the stuttering fluorescent light, the gray linoleum floor, and the one tiny window. *I wonder where you come from,* she thought. *I wonder why you ended up in this place.*

One time she'd asked him, in a fit of boldness, what the English assignment was. He'd just pointed to the board, where it said they were supposed to prepare for an in-class essay on *The Tempest,* but he looked as though he'd wanted to say something else. She knew he could talk; she'd heard him talk to other people. She prepared to give him an encouraging look, but when she met his eyes, which were the color of canned peas, she was suddenly swept away by an awkwardness so confounding that she cast her gaze to the floor and didn't pick it up again until the end of class. Usually she wasn't like that. She was a reasonably confident person. She knew who she was and where she fit. She'd grown up mostly among girls, but between student government and the ceramics studio and Marnie's two brothers, she had plenty of friends who were boys. None of them made her feel the way Daniel did.

And then there was the time, at the end of junior year, when she was cleaning out her locker. She was aching at the thought of not seeing him for the entire summer. She had parked her dad's rusted white Blazer badly, with two wheels up on the curb a couple of blocks from school. She had left piles of papers and books from her locker and a cardboard box of her pottery on the sidewalk while she tried to gentle the door open.

She saw Daniel out of the corner of her eye at first. He wasn't walking anywhere or carrying anything. He was just standing still with his arms dangling at his sides, gazing at her with that lost expression on his face. His face was sad and a bit remote, as though he was looking inside himself as much as he was looking out at her. She turned and met his eyes, and neither of them jumped away this time. He stood there as if he was trying to remember something.

The ordinary part of her wanted to wave or make a comment that seemed clever or memorable, but another part of her just held her breath. It seemed that they really knew each other, not simply that she had thought of him obsessively for a year. It seemed that he was trusting her to just stand there for a moment, as though there were so many important things they could have said to each other that they didn't need to say any of them at all. He looked uncertain and walked away, and she wondered what it meant. Later she tried to explain it to Marnie as evidence of a true connection, but Marnie tossed it away as another "non-event."

Marnie felt that she was in charge of taming Lucy's expectations and had even adopted a special mantra for the purpose: "If he liked you, you would know it," she said constantly, a phrase Lucy suspected she'd read in a book.

It wasn't just that Lucy wanted to help him. She wasn't as selfless as that. She was madly attracted to him. She was attracted to all the normal things and then weird things, too, like the back of his neck and his thumbs on the edge of his desk and the way his hair stuck out on one side like a little wing over his ear. She caught his smell once, and it made her dizzy. She couldn't fall asleep that night.

And the truth was that he offered her something that no other boy in the school could: He didn't know Dana. Dana had always been a "handful," as her mother decorously put it, but when they were young she had been Lucy's hero. She was the smartest, fastest-talking person Lucy knew, and she was always brave. Brave and also reckless. When Lucy got in trouble for something, even for something dumb, like tracking mud into the house or spilling ketchup on the floor, Dana would take the blame. She did it even when Lucy begged her not to, because she said she didn't mind blame and Lucy did.

Dana became notorious when Lucy was in fifth grade and she was in ninth. Lucy didn't understand what all the whispering among the older kids and grown-ups meant at first, but she knew there was something to be ashamed of. "I had your sister," one or another of her teachers would always say significantly. Certain kids wouldn't come to her house anymore, or even invite her to theirs, and she understood that her family had done something wrong without really knowing what it was. Only Marnie was her unwavering friend.

By seventh grade Dana was the "Go Ask Alice" of the school, the cautionary tale, and her parents were the ones people endlessly speculated about. Did they drink? Were there drugs in the house? Had the mother worked when the girls were young? The speculation usually ended with somebody saying, "They *seem* nice enough."

Her parents took it all with heads bent so low it was like an invitation for more. Their shame was boundless, and it was easier getting blamed than doing nothing at all. Dana held her head high, but the rest of them walked around with a black eye and an apology.

161

Lucy tried to be loyal sometimes and other times wished her last name was Johnson, of which there were fourteen in the school. She tried to talk to Dana, and when it made no difference she convinced herself she didn't care. How many times could you give up on someone you loved? "Lucy's a different kind of Broward," she overheard her math teacher say to the guidance counselor when she entered high school, and she felt horrible for how fiercely she clung to it. She thought if she tried hard enough she could make amends.

Dana fell back a few grades for lack of attendance and every other possible crime that wasn't academic: drugs, violence, giving blow jobs in the boys' bathroom. Lucy once saw the envelope on her father's desk declaring Dana a National Merit Scholarship finalist based on her SAT scores. It was strange, the things Dana chose to do.

She dropped out for good on the second-to-last day of school, just a week before she would have graduated. She appeared again on graduation day and in the midst of "Pomp and Circumstance" made her dramatic exit. Daniel was possibly the only boy Lucy knew who hadn't seen Dana tearing off her clothes on the school's front lawn, surrounded by medics trying not to get their eyes scratched out as they carted her to the hospital for the last time.

Dana overdosed on Thanksgiving that year and went into a coma. She died quietly on Christmas. She was buried on New Year's Eve at a ceremony attended by the family and Marnie, her two surviving grandparents, and her crazy aunt from Duluth. The single representative from the school was Mr. Margum, who was the physics teacher and the youngest member of the faculty. Lucy wasn't sure if he came because Dana had aced his class or maybe given him a blow job or both.

Among the complicated legacy of Dana, the most tangible thing she left was a four-foot corn snake named Sawmill, and Lucy got stuck with it. What else could she do? Her mother wasn't going to take care of it. Week after week she thawed the frozen mice and fed them to him with abiding discomfort. She dutifully changed his warming light. She thought maybe Sawmill would die without the animating spirit of Dana in his life, and one time she saw a desiccated, inert version of him in his glass box and for a moment believed—with a mixture of horror and relief—that he had. But it turned out he had only molted. He was lounging in his hollow log, looking fresher than ever. Lucy suddenly remembered the dry gray skins Dana had thumbtacked to her wall, her only effort toward home decorating.

Eleventh grade was the first year Lucy allowed herself to be something other than Dana's sister. Because she was pretty, the boys forgot faster than the girls, but they all came around eventually.

Lucy was elected junior class secretary in the late fall. Two of her clay pieces, a vase and a bowl, were chosen for a statewide art show. Every moment of freedom or success was outmatched by a moment of guilt and grief. She hated that she wanted anything from them, but she did.

"You know, Lu, I don't have a single friend at that school," she remembered Dana telling her once, as though that was a real surprise.

"HE'S PROBABLY NOT even going to show up," Marnie announced over the phone as they were both getting ready for the Senior Ball, the final event of high school.

"He will if he wants to get his signed diploma," Lucy pointed out before she hung up the phone and went back to her closet.

Marnie called a second time. "Even if he does show, it's not like he's going to talk to you."

"Maybe I'll talk to him."

Lucy carefully took her new lavender silk slip dress out of her closet and undid the plastic. She laid it with care across her bed while she changed from a regular bra into a lacy cream-colored one. She painted her toenails pale pink and spent a full fifteen minutes at the sink trying to clean the clay and gardening soil out from under her fingernails. She used a curling iron, knowing the curls would fall out of her straight, slippery hair within the hour. As she drew black eyeliner along the edge of her top eyelid, she pictured Daniel watching her and wondering why she was stabbing herself in the eyeball with a pencil.

She often thought of that. Embarrassingly often. Whatever she was doing, she would imagine Daniel there with his thoughts and opinions. And though they'd never really spoken, she always had a clear idea of what he would think. He wouldn't like a lot of makeup, for instance. The blow-dryer would strike him as loud and pointless, and her eyelash curler like a torture device. He liked her sunflower seeds but not her Diet Pepsi. As her iPod shuffled her songs, she knew the ones he liked and the ones he thought were stupid.

He liked her dress, she decided, as she pulled it carefully over her head and let the delicate fabric settle over her body. That's why she'd picked it.

Marnie called again. "You should have gone with Stephen. He asked you nicely."

"I didn't want to go with Stephen," she said.

"Well, Stephen would bring you flowers. He'd pose for good pictures."

"I don't like him. What would I want those pictures for?" She didn't mention the main trouble with Stephen, which was that Marnie obviously admired him.

"And he'd dance with you. Stephen's a good dancer. Daniel's not going to dance with you. He's not going to care if you are there or not."

"Maybe he'll care. You don't know that."

"He won't. He's had a lot of chances to care, and he hasn't."

After Lucy hung up the phone for the last time she stood in front of the mirror. She did rue the lack of flowers a little. She clipped three small violets from the pots on her windowsill, two purple and one pink. She attached them to a hairpin and tucked them an inch above her ear. That was better.

Marnie came to the front door at a quarter to eight. Lucy could read the expression on her mom's face as she came down the stairs. Her mother had been guardedly wishing for some version of Stephen, a handsome guy in a tux wielding a corsage, and not just Marnie again, in her ripped black stockings. She'd had two lovely fair-haired daughters and not one eager boy in a tuxedo to show for it. To look like Lucy had been enough in her day.

Lucy felt the old pang. Now she knew what she wanted those pictures for. Her mother could use them to remember a better outcome than she'd had. Lucy appeased herself with her usual litany of guilt reducers: She wasn't taking drugs. She wasn't piercing her tongue or getting a tattoo of a spider on her neck. She was wearing a lavender dress and pink toenail polish and violets in her hair. She couldn't do everything right.

"Oh, God," Marnie said when she looked Lucy over. "Did you have to do all that?"

"All what?"

"Never mind."

"All what?"

"Nothing."

Lucy had tried too hard. That was it. She looked down at her dress and at her gold shoes. "This might be the last time I see him," she said plaintively. "I don't know what will happen after this. I need to make him remember me."

"I HATE THIS SONG. Let's go outside."

Lucy followed Marnie out of the school auditorium. Marnie hated every song, and Lucy creaked back and forth on her gold shoes, watching the dark red ring of lipstick on the filter of Marnie's cigarette. Marnie hunched down to relight, and Lucy saw the tender yellow roots at her part, pushing away the dyed-dark hair.

"I'm not seeing Daniel," Marnie said, more grumpy than triumphant.

"Who'd Stephen come with?" Lucy asked, meaner than she should've been.

"Shut up," Marnie said, because she had her disappointments, too.

Lucy did shut up for a while, watching the smoke climb and dissipate. She thought of Daniel's diploma left on the table along the wall of the gymnasium, and it felt like a rebuke to her. He really wasn't going to come. He really didn't care about her. Lucy felt as though her makeup was stiffening on her face. She wanted to wash it off. She looked down at her dress, which cost her an entire semester of Saturdays working at the bagel shop. What if she never saw him again? The thought gave her an almost panicked feeling. This could not be all there was.

"What was that?" Marnie turned her head abruptly.

Lucy heard it, too. There was shouting inside the school, and then a scream. You hear plenty of screams in the vicinity of a high school party, but this was one that made you stop.

Marnie stood with a look of surprise Lucy rarely caught on her face. People were piling up at the main doors, and you could hear the shouting. Lucy startled at the sound of glass shattering. Something was really wrong.

Who do you think of when glass is breaking and people are screaming real screams? That was a telling thing. Marnie was right there and her mother was home, so Lucy thought of Daniel. What if he was in there somewhere? The crowd was piling up thick and wild at the main doors, and she needed to know what was going on.

She went in through the side door. The hallway was dark, so she ran toward the shouting. She stopped as she intersected with the senior hallway. She heard more glass breaking in the distance. She saw dark streaks on the floor and instinctively knew what it was. More blood pooled and rolled down the senior hallway, and she would have thought, she observed numbly, that that floor was flat. She took a few steps and froze. Somebody, a boy, was lying there mostly in the dark and everybody else was running away. It was his blood that was creeping down the hall. *"What is going on?"* she shouted after them.

She felt for her cell phone in her bag with shaking hands. By the time she'd opened it she heard the sirens, and there were many of them all at once. Somebody grabbed her arm and pulled at her, but she shook him off. The blood crept toward the toe of her gold shoe. Somebody stepped in it and ran away, making shoe prints on the linoleum, and that just seemed wrong.

She made her way toward the body on the ground, trying not to walk in his blood. She leaned down to see his face. It was a boy in the junior class, a face she recognized but didn't know. She crouched beside him and touched his arm. He was groaning with each breath. He was alive, at least. "Are you all right?" It seemed obvious he wasn't. "Help is coming," she assured him weakly.

Suddenly she heard an explosion of shouting and footsteps coming toward her as the police arrived. They were yelling at everybody. They blocked the doors and told everybody to calm down, though they themselves were not calm.

"Is there an ambulance?" she said. Not loud enough, so she said it again. She hadn't realized she was crying.

Two policemen rushed to the boy, and she stepped back. There was another eruption of shouting into radios. They made way for the EMS guys to get through.

"Is he okay?" she asked, too quietly to make any difference. She backed up farther. She couldn't see anything anymore.

At that moment a policewoman pulled at her roughly. "You're not going anywhere," she commanded, even though Lucy wasn't going anywhere. She directed her down the science hall and pointed to a door on the right. "Go in there and stay until we can get a detective in to talk to you. Don't move, do you hear me?"

She pushed open the door to the chemistry lab where she had done experiments on the Bunsen burners in tenth grade.

Through the windows she first saw all the red from the lights of the police cars. She waded through dark chairs and tables to see out. There were probably ten police cars parked at odd angles on the patch of grass at the back of school where they spent free periods in good weather. When the lights flashed over it she could see how the tires had chewed up the grass, and that seemed like a further dire thing.

She made her way to the classroom sink more by memory than sight. She could have found the light switch, but she didn't feel like exposing herself to all the people bustling outside the windows. She turned on the faucet and bent forward, washing away makeup and tears. She dried her face with a stiff brown paper towel. Her violets drooped. She'd thought the room was empty until she turned around and saw the figure sitting at a desk in the corner, and it scared her. She walked closer, trying to adjust her eyes to the darkness.

"Who is that?" she asked in a voice just above a whisper.

"Daniel."

She stopped. The red glow filled in parts of his face.

"Sophia," he said.

She came closer so he could see who she was. "No, it's Lucy." Her voice shook a little. There was a boy bleeding in the hallway, and she felt a gathering disappointment that he still didn't know her.

"Come sit down." He wore a stoic expression, a look of resignation, as if he would rather she were Sophia.

She skimmed along the edge of the room, picking over chairs and jackets and bags kids had stowed there. Her dress felt insubstantial for this kind of night. He was sitting back against the wall in one of those desk/chair combinations with his feet crossed as though he was waiting for something.

She wasn't sure how close to sit, but he pulled a desk/chair toward him so the two right-handed desks faced each other like yin and yang. She shivered as she got close. She felt the goose bumps on her bare arms. Self-consciously she pulled the violets from her hair.

"You're cold," he said. He glanced at the little flowers on the desk.

"I'm okay," she said. Most of the goose bumps were owing to him.

He looked around at the piles on the stools and chairs and desktops. He pulled out a white sweatshirt with a falcon on it and held it out to her. She put it over her shoulders but did not contend with the sleeves or zipper.

"Do you know what happened?" she asked, leaning forward, her hair brushing past her shoulders so it almost touched his hands.

He spread his hands out flat on the desk as she'd seen him do many times in English class. They were the hands of a man and not a boy. He seemed to be steadying them for something. "Some juniors crashed and vandalized the senior lounge and hallway. A couple of them had knives, and there was a fight. I think two of them got cut and one kid got stabbed."

"I saw him. He was lying on the ground."

He nodded. "He'll be all right. It's his leg. It'll bleed, but he'll be all right."

"Really?" She wondered how he knew.

"Did EMS get there yet?"

She nodded.

"Then yes. He'll be fine." He looked as though he was thinking about something else.

"That's good." She believed him whether he deserved it or not, and it made her feel better. Her teeth were chattering, so she closed her mouth to make it stop.

He leaned down and lifted something from a bag on the floor. It was a bottle of bourbon, half full. "Somebody left their stash." He went over to the sink and took a plastic cup from the stack. "Here."

He was pouring it before she said yes or no. He put it on the desk right in front of her, leaning so close she could feel his warmth. She felt breathless and light in her head. She put her hand to her warm throat, knowing it was turning red, as it did in moments of deep agitation.

"I didn't realize you were here," she said, forgetting to think how she revealed herself by saying so.

He nodded. "I came late. I heard the screaming all the way from the parking lot. I wanted to see what was going on."

She would have taken a sip of the bourbon, but her hands were shaking and she didn't want him to see. Maybe he understood this, because he leaned away from her toward the counter, where he switched on a burner. She watched the dots of fire flicker around the rim before the flame took hold. It reflected off the glass door and made a faint quivery light through the room. She took a quick sip and felt the sting and burn of it in her cold mouth. She tried not to wince at the fumes. It wasn't exactly her custom to drink whiskey.

"Will you have some?" she asked when he'd settled back into the desk/chair contraption. His knees brushed against hers. She didn't think he'd been intending to drink any. But he looked at her, and he looked at the cup. He reached for it, and she watched in amazement as he put it to his lips just where her lips had been and took a long sip. She'd imagined he might pour himself a cup but never that he'd share hers. What would Marnie say to that? This was intimacy she couldn't quite believe. She was sitting with him, talking with him, drinking with him. It was happening so fast she couldn't quite take it in.

She took another sip, recklessly. If he saw the shaking, she didn't care. Her hand was where his hand was and her lips over his lips.

Do you have any idea how much I've loved you?

He sat back again. He tipped his head to the side and studied her face. Their knees touched. She waited for him to say something, but he was quiet.

She squeezed the plastic cup nervously in her hand, bending the circle to an oval and back. "I thought the year would end and we would all go our separate ways and we would never have talked to each other," she said bravely. She felt like her words echoed in the silence, and hated being stuck with them for so long. She wished he would say something to cover them over.

He smiled at her. She thought she had never seen his smile. He was beautiful. "I wouldn't have let that happen," he said.

"You wouldn't?" She was so genuinely surprised she couldn't help asking. "Why not?"

He continued to study her, as though he had many things to say and wasn't sure he was ready to say them. "I've been wanting to talk to you," he said slowly. "I wasn't sure . . . when the right time would be."

In a completely juvenile and heady way, she wished Marnie could have heard him say that.

"But this is a strange night," he went on. "Maybe not the best time. Tonight I just wanted to make sure you were all right."

"You did?" She was worried her face was so eager as to be pitiful.

He smiled in that same way again. "Of course."

She took another sip of bourbon and giddily passed it to him as if they were old friends. Did he have any idea how much time she had spent thinking about him and fantasizing about him and parsing his every glance and gesture? "What did you want to talk to me about?"

"Well." He was trying to measure something about her; she didn't know what. He took another long swig. "I probably shouldn't be doing this. I don't know." He shook his head, and his face was serious. She wasn't sure if he meant drinking bourbon or talking to her.

"Shouldn't be doing what?"

He looked at her so hard it almost scared her. She wanted nothing more in the world than to have him stare into her eyes, but this was too much to take in. It was like buckets of water spilling off of parched soil.

"I've thought about this a lot. There are so many things I've wanted to say to you. I don't want to"—he paused to choose his words—"overwhelm you."

She had never had a boy talk to her like that. There was no cover of bullshit, no flirtation, no added charm, but his look was searing. He was different from anyone she had known.

She swallowed hard to keep herself down. She felt she could turn inside out and show him her kidneys if she wasn't careful. She would hold herself together, but she wouldn't leave him out there on his own. "Do you know how much I've thought about you?"

They were sitting knees to knees, pressing them together, so when he split his legs hers went right through until they were practically joined. Her knee was nearly in his crotch, and his was in hers. Her knee was bare, and his knee was deep under her dress, pressed against her underwear, and her nerves were thrumming. She had a feeling of disbelief. She was suspicious that her imagination was choreographing this out of pure desire and that it wasn't really happening.

"Have you?" he asked. She suddenly knew, just knew, that he was soaking her in, that he was as parched as she was.

He reached out and put his hand on the back of her neck and pulled her forward. She drew in her breath, astonished that he would put his mouth on hers. He kissed her. She lost herself in his breath and his warmth and his smell. She leaned so far forward that she felt the edge of the desk cutting into her rib cage under her breasts and her heart slamming against it.

His arm hit the cup of bourbon, and it fell to the floor. She vaguely felt the liquid splash and puddle under her foot and didn't care. She meant to stay in his kiss until she died if necessary, but she felt something strange, a strange sensation barreling toward her, a heavy foreboding. She was able to ignore it for a while, until it crashed into her all at once.

It was a sensation of feeling and remembering at the same time, two explosions colliding and expanding. It was like déjà vu but far more intense. She felt dizzy and suddenly afraid. She opened her eyes and pulled back from him. She looked into his eyes. She felt tears on her face, wholly different from her earlier tears. "Who are you?" she whispered.

His eyes seemed to dilate and refocus. "Do you remember?"

She could not make herself see in front of her. The room spun so violently she closed her eyes and he was there, too, behind her eyes, as though from her memory. He was lying on a bed and she was looking down at him, and she felt an undertow of despair she didn't understand.

She felt him now holding both her hands, she realized, and hard. When she opened her eyes his expression was so intense she wanted to look away. "Do you remember?" He looked as though his life depended on her answer.

She felt scared. She had another scene invading her mind that she couldn't place. It was him, but in a strange setting, not anywhere she knew. She felt as if she was fully awake and dreaming at the same time. "Did I know you before?" She felt sure it was true, and also that it couldn't be. She had a terror of not knowing quite where she was.

"Yes." She saw that there were tears in his eyes.

He pulled her out from the desk and held her standing up so her whole body was clutched to his. She felt a rocking against her chest, and she didn't know if it was her heart or his. "You are Sophia. Do you know that?" Her head was pressed into his neck, and she felt dampness on top of her head.

If he wasn't holding her, she didn't think she could stand up. She felt herself slipping. She didn't know where she was or who she was, and she didn't know what she remembered. She wondered if the bourbon was acting as some kind of hallucinogen or if she was just losing her mind.

Is this what it was like? Dana had loved to be out of control, but Lucy hated it. She pictured an ambulance coming to get her. She thought of her mother.

She pulled roughly away from him. "There is something wrong with me," she said tearfully.

He didn't want to let her go, but he saw the whiteness of her face and the fear. "What do you mean?"

"I have to go."

"Sophia." She realized he had two fistfuls of her dress, and he wasn't letting them go.

"No, it's Lucy," she said. Was he crazy? He was. He was confused and thought she was someone else. He was having some kind of psychosis. He was so crazy he was making her crazy, too.

She suddenly felt an overwhelming sense of danger. She cared about him too much, and he was a dangerous person to love. He wouldn't love her back. He'd suck her into pure confusion where he thought she was someone else. And she would want so much to believe him that she wouldn't know who she was anymore.

"Please let go."

"But. Wait. *Sophia.* You do remember."

"No. I don't. You're scaring me. I don't know. I don't know what you are talking about." She sobbed between the words.

She felt his hands shaking. She couldn't look at the despair in his face. "I wish I could tell you everything. I wish you knew. Please let me try to explain."

She pulled away so hard her dress tore down the front. She looked down and then at him. He looked surprised and horrified that he was still holding the fabric in his hands.

"Oh, God. I'm sorry."

He tried to put the sweatshirt around her to cover her up. "I'm so sorry," he said. He wouldn't take his arms from her. He wouldn't let her go. "I'm so sorry. I love you. Do you know that?" He was holding her, pressing his face desperately in her hair. "I always have."

She wrested herself away from him. She caught the desk with her leg and sent it backward. She tripped over chairs and bags to get to the door. She couldn't be loved like this. Not even her. Not even by him.

"You don't," she said without turning around. "You don't even know who I am."

She didn't remember getting to the front doors of the school, but a policeman found her there. She was crying and couldn't find a way out because all the doors were locked. That's what the cop told her mother when she came to get her, but Lucy honestly didn't remember any of it.

from

The Postmistress

by

Sarah Blake

**"This compelling story is the perfect answer to that
request, 'I want a really good book I can get lost in.'"**
—*The Boston Globe*

The Postmistress *is a tale of two worlds—one shattered by
violence, the other willfully naive—and of two women whose
job is to deliver the news, yet who find themselves unable to
do so. Through their eyes, and the eyes of everyday people
caught in history's tide, it examines how we tell each other
stories, and how we bear the fact of war as we live ordinary
lives.*

*"A beautifully written, thought-provoking novel that I'm
telling everyone I know to read."*
　　　　　　　　　—*Kathryn Stockett, author of* The Help

15.

ONE OF THE impossible absurdities of war was that the trains between countries still ran. Like mechanized ants, the trains continued, and a person could get from Dover across the Channel to Calais in a morning, and on into Paris by the end of that day. That and the fact that the northern French countryside bloomed a light fairy green could drive a person mad. *Not at war, not at war,* the train clacked over the rails the following morning. The Norman fields had been turned and planted, and the poplars spiked against the pale sky. Men, loosely wrapped, worked in the fields, paying no attention to the passing train.

The train reached Paris at a little after six. Montmartre's dome rounded above the sharp roofs in the near distance. Frankie had pulled the window down all the way, and spring crept into the compartment, even as the train slid slowly past the outlying market towns. A woman on a bicycle kept pace with the train, and Frankie watched her ride past the swastika flapping from the flagpole in the village square, so upright on her seat, her head covered in a scarf, so *French*.

She didn't have much time to find the train for Berlin, but

there was little trouble getting on. She climbed onto the second to last compartment and settled herself into a seat as the train started up and Paris fell slowly away.

When the train passed out of France into occupied Belgium, the engine was uncoupled and changed, and the travelers sat in the dark for hours, making it feel like another bloody funk hole, Frankie thought. The sun had set long ago and the blackout curtains pulled in the windows of the tiny station, clear evidence that the British bombers had penetrated this far.

The train crossed into Germany, pushing forward into the dark, the telegraph wires glinting like needles in the night. Sometime before dawn, they stopped at what looked like a crossing and an order was given just below Frankie's compartment window, and then repeated farther down the line. She lifted her shade and saw what looked like a ghost army in the night, the dim moon glinting off chin straps and gun barrels. There must have been a hundred men down there, all of them silent, waiting to move. The locomotive shuddered and sighed.

As they drew nearer to Berlin, the train emptied of ordinary people. Few were traveling so far east. By the time they reached the city the following morning, Frankie was alone in her compartment. She sat a minute before getting off. The air was lovely outside and, as in Paris, she could just see the broad flank of the avenues stretched away from the train station and the slight green against the marble buildings, all of which dislocated the present. She stood and pulled her bag down from the rack above her head, grabbed the recorder, and emerged onto the platform where what looked like hundreds of people were waiting. She turned around. The only train she could see was the one she had just left. It wasn't so much a line of people as a wave, held in check by the shut doors of the cars. In these exhausted, fearful groupings the present returned. Some faces stared at her as she passed, and she nodded hello. They dropped their eyes as though she were dangerous.

The few other passengers had gotten off as well, and at the end of the platform the line for passport control began to thicken. She'd be glad of a bath and a drink, she thought, getting into the line that snaked toward her. A bath, a drink, and then a long, long walk into the city. The safe-transit pass had been read and refolded at each of the border checkpoints, and her passport stamped. She set down her bag and the recorder and kept them between her legs, handing over the letter.

"How long?"

"Overnight." Frankie smiled at the officer. He was tidy and round. He looked up at her with startlingly black eyes.

He took her papers, looked at them, and spread them out on the table. His fingernails were bitten to the quick. "No, Fräulein." He shook his head.

She frowned and leaned over the table. "What do you mean?"

He looked up at her, pleasantly. "If you plan to leave Berlin tomorrow, you must stay here and take the next train."

"Why is that?"

"There is no room," he answered blandly, handing her papers back to her.

"I'm a reporter," she said as evenly as she could.

"Ah?" He looked her up and down, his eyes without light and letting none in.

"And what is it you are reporting?"

"On the trains out of Berlin."

"For what purpose?"

"To give my country a feel for the wartime conditions."

"Conditions have never been better."

"Exactly." She looked at him.

"No, Fräulein." And he gestured to the man in uniform behind him.

"I'm American."

"We have plenty of Americans already." He shrugged. The second man came to stand beside her.

"May I cable my office?"

His lip curled. "Your office? Fräulein, if you wish to ride the trains, this will be the last one out for a very long time."

"Why's that?"

He shrugged and waved her papers. She took them. His raisin eyes swung slowly up to hers. "Good journey, Fräulein."

She bent and picked up her two cases, and turned back into the crowd.

The heavy smell of fear hung in the close air of the waiting room. Several people looked up when Frankie entered, but their attention was on the officer beside her. He might make an announcement. With every hour stalled, not moving, the exit visas—clearly stamped with the date by which they had to leave the country—went closer to expiring and they had not yet even begun the journey. Each person held hard-won transit papers as well, allowing them to pass through on their way to the boats. A problem with either meant that at any point they could be turned away, refused entry, sent back. So they had to get on the train. The train Frankie had just left stood idle on the track behind her. Through the glass right in front of them stood the voyage out. It sat there, guarded by two soldiers, guns slung over their shoulders.

The washroom door was surrounded by women; Frankie went to join them.

"How long have you been waiting here?" Frankie asked in German.

One of the women turned around. "Since morning. The train was supposed to leave at ten."

It was nearly two o'clock. The journey had begun, Frankie realized, half-writing the script. *The journey begins on an empty platform with no train in sight.* The door of the washroom opened in front of her, and a tiny curly blond-headed woman clutching a child by the hand emerged. Her blouse strained over her pregnant belly; she had the scattered, wide-eyed look of someone waiting for the next blow. She kept tight hold of her boy, though, and steered him through the women. Frankie turned and followed her to see what the husband looked like. But the woman sank down into a spot on one of the benches, evidently held for her by a matronly older woman in a black cotton dress. No husband. Frankie turned back. Hers might be the story to follow. A military band had begun to play in the cavernous center of the station, and Frankie felt the drums in her bones.

Suddenly, the scene through the window burst into life. Several soldiers ran down the platform, signaling the two already there to move to the front. A fuel car backed down the parallel track, its engineer a great blond man calling jokes down to his comrades; everyone burst into laughter. The drums stopped and the steady thrum of the diesel filled the station with life. The mood around Frankie lightened, too; perhaps *now* they were leaving. People began to stand up, holding their possessions to their chests, watching the one train couple with the other, giving it fuel.

From down the avenue came the sound of whistles and the motors of several engines. Frankie counted six trucks, pulling right into the station alongside the tracks. Out of them jumped men in uniform, boys mostly. Within minutes, the platform in front of her was crowded with them, standing awkwardly around waiting, as were the people in flight, watching through the glass. Despite, or perhaps because of, the audience in the waiting room, the young men seemed to Frankie to play at being soldiers, in the manner of schoolboys, strutting and smoking, clearly anxious to set off, to be sent into the thick of things. The opinion in the room where Frankie waited was that the soldiers were headed for the Russian border. There had been three call-ups in the last two weeks from central Berlin. Soldiers and tea and all the tinned meat left in the city, a woman with a thick lip and quiet watchful eyes commented to Frankie. Everything to Russia, she said regretfully. And the trains, a man put in beside her. All the trains, too.

Frankie glanced back at the bench where the mother and her little boy still sat, the boy asleep against his mother's arm. The woman was clearly on her own.

A sleek Daimler crept along the platform, leaving order behind as it passed. The boys became real soldiers, their shoulders back and their legs snapped together. An officer stepped out of the car and shouted some kind of encouragement, and then the line slackened and the boys stepped on the train. Within an hour, the waiting room stared again at an empty track. Frankie went to find some dinner and sat herself in the station café, watching the same blank track as those in the waiting room who would not leave their spots by the door. The boy was up on his feet in front of his mother now, slapping his hands together, trying for her gaze. Every so often, she'd look down at him, away from the train track. Sometimes she'd smile. Frankie decided against approaching her now, all of her attention strained toward the hoped-for train.

Around three a.m., a siren went off and a new train pulled into the station, much smaller than the one Frankie had ridden from Paris, this one only six cars, and everyone in the waiting room rose up and surged forward. There was no hanging back, no chance to let others take spots before her. The crowd moved in one panic-stricken wave toward the door of the waiting room, which someone had opened, and then gushed through onto the platform to halt at the gunmetal exterior of the cars. The doors were pulled shut and none of the lights were lit; it seemed unmanned at first to Frankie, and eerie in the dark. A man shouted something from the front of the train, and the family beside Frankie looked at her. Did you hear? She shook her head.

Then suddenly, like Aladdin's cave, the doors were thrown open. Again, the human wave gathered and Frankie felt herself lifted off her feet briefly. Someone cried out behind her, and over her shoulder she glimpsed the tiny mother and her toddler pressed against a man's back. Frankie shoved her overnight bag under her arm, freeing her to reach back and grab the boy's hand, pulling him up and against her out of the crush. *All right*, she said to him, *it's all right. Franz!* His mother shrieked. *I've got him! Je le tiens!* Frankie cried back. The mother grabbed Frankie's waist from behind, and all three of them were pushed forward and up the stairs into the train.

Frankie opened the first compartment, saw that there was a half-spot, and pushed her way in, putting the boy down between two men. *Here*, she pointed to the mother, who was panting, her breath coming in fast panicky claps, and the younger of the two men leapt up to give her his seat. She sank down onto the compartment seat; her little boy stood frozen, his eyes fixed on his mother's face. Her breathing was rapid and ragged. Frankie wished desperately she had water. "Put your head down," the older man suggested softly in German. He was heavyset but shaven. He was used to giving directions. Perhaps a teacher, thought Frankie. Why was he traveling alone? The mother didn't hear. "Head down." He stood up to grab her by the shoulders and force her head down. The train gave a lurch, knocking everyone in the compartment off balance. The man stumbled against Frankie, but then righted himself and spoke more gently to the young mother who looked up at him finally, nodded, and bent over.

Someone banged on the train window and Frankie looked up and saw the frantic face of a woman outside pressed against the glass, shouting at her. The train shifted and sighed and crept forward. The woman on the platform dropped her arm, but there was a relentless banging still on the car below the window. It became clear that the train was going to leave everyone on the platform behind and Frankie stared down into all those faces upturned to hers and knew she was looking at ghosts. They were not going to get out. A different train, on a different night perhaps. But this one was full, though everyone out there held a ticket, and a large enough train had been promised. They were drowning there right in front of her, within sight of the lifeboats, within sight of shore, and here she was, taking up a spot.

She whirled around to get out of the compartment, to get out of the train, to give someone, anyone else, her place.

"Let me pass," she cried to the older man sitting next to the compartment door, but as she reached for the handle, he closed his hand over hers.

She frowned. "Let me go."

He pointed at the door, and through it she looked into the backs of a handful of people pressed against the glass, and against them, in another row, stood more. The corridor outside was jammed with men and women. There was no getting out of the carriage. Oh God, she thought, turning around to face those outside, a sob rising in her chest. And the train started off, gathered speed, and pulled faster away from the people on the platform below, and its whistle blew.

Frankie sank down onto the case of the disk recorder, her suitcase on her lap in the dirty spot of open carpet between the two benches, and she leaned her head against the door. There were seven of them and the child jammed into the compartment. And none of them spoke. The mother's breathing had quieted and slowed. Her little boy pressed against her and watched the others. There was no room for him on her lap, but he would not squeeze onto the bench beside her. For a while the train's motion and patches of moonlight along the blackened city outskirts held everyone quiet, the journey started at last.

Get on a refugee train, Murrow had instructed; and though it was obscene, absurd of her at this point in time, having seen so much, she had harbored the impossible illusion that "refugee train" meant people who were saved. These people might as well have leapt. No one was safe, none was saved. Until they got to the end, they were simply on the run.

"Fräulein?" The younger of the two men was the first to break the silence in the car. Frankie looked up. He was pointing to her and then to his seat. He wore an ill-fitting hand-knit sweater pulled over a knotted tie, and the hand he held out was smudged with ink. "No, thanks," she said, shaking her head. He lifted his hand and smiled at her, as if to say, well perhaps later then, and she smiled back at him. He nodded and crossed his arms over his chest, leaning back against the compartment wall, evidently satisfied. He had offered. The knot in Frankie's

stomach relaxed just slightly in the wake of that familiar gesture. All of them, there in the dark, heading away from Berlin, traveling out, could offer each other a seat, could still offer
something, and still refuse.

Across from him, nearest the window, a round-faced woman
somewhere in her middle age released her attention on the rest
of them and pressed into the corner. She rested her head against
the window frame and closed her eyes, her chin settling in her
several collars. A blue jersey strained across the pointed tips of
a brown wool suit jacket, and on top of that a darker blue, also
wool, shirt and sweater. Even with her eyes closed, she gripped
the handles of the battered leather case on her lap. Beside her
sat a very pretty young woman, whom Frankie at first took to
be the older woman's daughter, but it was clear soon enough
that she was traveling with the boy beside her. They were both
dark-eyed and fair-skinned, and the sister's curls flashed out
from her tight cap, dancing with the motion of the train. No
more than twelve, he had watched Frankie refuse the man's seat
with curious attention.

"American?" He looked down at her eagerly.

She nodded.

"We are going there," he pronounced.

His sister put her hand on his knee to stop it jiggling.

He turned to her, frowning. She put her fingers to her lips.
Frankie smiled at him and caught the imperceptible shift of
the older woman in the corner, drawing herself farther away
from the girl. The moonlight caught her full in the face and her
eyes blinked open once, then firmly shut. The sister took her
brother's hand quietly in hers and leaned her head back against
the compartment wall. In the frightened, exhausted silence, the
tiny boy across from them had fallen asleep on his feet, clamped

between his mother's legs and resting his head on the enormous swell of her pregnant belly. This close, Frankie saw how dirty his hair was and matted, the backs of his legs grayed with soot. The mother was no more than a child herself, and Frankie watched as she turned to look into the blank black of the night train windows, the sleeping face of her boy turned up to her like a little skyless moon.

For the fourth night in a row, Frankie settled herself in the thick dark between sleepers and, like her companions, tried to doze. But as soon as she shut her eyes, the doctor's big body flipped effortlessly off his feet into the air before her. She shuddered and opened her eyes. The old woman in the corner was crying without sound, tears streaking down her cheeks. Her hands still held on to the bag in her lap, resting like a stone. The boy and girl beside her had fallen asleep on each other. The young man who had offered his seat slept with his arms across his chest, his head down as though he was considering a question.

She fingered the clasp on the black case beneath her. She ought to take it out and start asking questions in her simple German: *Where are you going? Where have you come from? What happened?* She ought to focus her attention on the mother, get the beginnings of the story, get her voice on the disk at the outset of the journey. Although the brother and sister might be equally good to concentrate the story on. Frankie watched the older man watching out the window. She wondered whom he had left behind. And for the first time in her career, she wondered whether she had the guts to ask him. *Seek Truth and Report It,* the journalist's code instructed. *Seek Truth. Report It.* And *Minimize Harm.* Every one of the sleepers around her must have left someone behind. And she thought of the desperate faces of the people who hadn't made it onto this train. Minimize Harm? She shuddered. Let the sleepers sleep. Tomorrow would be soon enough to begin.

Two hours later, the train slowed and then pulled into a tiny blacked-out village, whose station was no more than a wooden sign pounded into a short field of flattened grass and a bench facing the tracks. Frankie saw the single light of a watchman's lantern glowing from the bench like a yellow eye. Everyone in the compartment sat up and pulled their papers out, readying for the scrutiny. Their compartment was in the middle of the train, and it took over an hour for the inspector to reach it. The fear was infectious, heavy as a blanket. The progress was agonizing. Why was it so slow? In the car next door, they could hear raised voices followed by abrupt silence. Their door swung open and an old man with a torch stood in the opening, his jaw slack. Just an old man doing a job, thought Frankie, handing her papers up to him without any visible interest or ire.

"American?" He squinted. She nodded. He didn't look at Murrow's letter; he took her passport, turned it over to see the insignia, then handed it back. He lifted his torch and looked at the boy whose eyes flared enormous in the light, then at the mother, and the old man snapped his fingers for papers, though once in his hands he hardly looked at them. The door closed after him and left them all in an uncertain silence. That was it? They sat together in the dark listening to the opening and closing of the rest of the compartments in their carriage.

"You are good luck," the older man said slowly in the quiet after the train resumed. The dawn was breaking in the near fields and a low spring morning arose, the slanted red coloring the stubble outside. They had crossed the first hurdle, but they were still in Germany.

"I beg your pardon?" Frankie was aware that the old woman in the corner had opened her eyes and was listening to them.

But the man only shrugged. The brother and sister had fallen back asleep, and the boy's lips had fallen open in a soft round.

"Where are you heading?" she asked the man in German.

"Lisbon." He nodded. He had been lucky, he said. He had not made it onto the previous two trains. His exit visa expired in one week. The fingers on the hand he held up were stubby and well-worn. Not a teacher—Frankie changed her mind—a shopkeeper, a butcher. Someone with a trade.

She smiled. "What is your name?"

"Werner Buchman," he replied. The woman across from him closed her eyes, as though releasing hold.

By the afternoon, the train had slowed and stopped in three isolated towns. Each time, the police boarded the train and made their way through the thick clot of people, one by one. No one could leave the stations, and during one stop, Frankie made her way along the platform, all the way to the barrier, and looked through it into a village market day. Out here, far from the city, there were potatoes and new onions. A woman held three potatoes in her gloved hand and looked up at Frankie across the way. The May sun glinted off the metal buttons of her coat. Behind her, the poplars were greened on the top, a light girlish green.

By the third stop at Leipzig, the group in Frankie's car had noticeably relaxed, and Frankie suspected that Werner had been right, that because she was in the car, the others were passed over lightly. The tiny mother was smiling at her boy who had crawled over to the young man in the sweater, now on the floor in Frankie's spot, and taken the piece of string he had tied to a sweet, pulling it back and forward as though teasing a kitten. The boy sucked on the sweet and leaned against his mother.

The brother and sister played cards, and the sister hummed to herself as she held hers. The little boy had wet himself, but the window was pulled down and the smell of mown grass from outside made it unexpectedly barnlike in the car. They crossed into the Black Forest as the sun set. With luck they'd make it to Strasbourg and the French border by ten or eleven. Then Lyon, Toulouse, and the day after tomorrow, to the Spanish border at Bayonne. From there one could count on two solid days across Spain and into Portugal to arrive at the sea and the boats at Lisbon. Four days from here, if all went as hoped.

Frankie reached down and opened the lid on the recorder. The two boys stared at her. She'd start with the mother and the little boy, she decided. And she'd start slow.

"Wie heißt du?" Frankie smiled over at the toddler, turning the switch. "What is your name?"

He stared back at her. His mother poked him idly with her finger. He took the sweet from his mouth. "Franz." He was very solemn.

"Franz Hofmann," his mother whispered.

He started off after the name. "Franz Hof . . ."

The brother put down his cards. "Franz Hofmann," he said to the little boy. "Go on."

But Franz shook his head.

"And you?" Frankie asked the sister, in her rudimentary German. "Speak into here," she motioned. "Say your name."

"Inga?" said the sister, shyly. "Inga Borg?" The brother laughed and took his turn, pronouncing the English words slowly, as though he beat them on a drum. "I am Litman."

"Where are you from?" Frankie asked.

The boy turned to his sister. Watching, Frankie wasn't sure

whether he didn't understand or if he was frightened by the question.

"We have papers," his sister said to Frankie in German.

"Of course." Frankie nodded to assure her. Then she leaned forward and said to the recorder in English, "This is Frankie Bard, traveling south from Berlin on the Deutsche Reichs- bahn. The sound you hear is the train making good time on the tracks." Inga watched her. "I have with me a brother and sister, Inga and Litman Borg. They look to be about seventeen and twelve years old, traveling alone. Tell me, where are you two traveling to?" She repeated the question softly in German.

"Lisbon," Inga answered.

"And where to, after that?"

"America."

"And where have you come from?"

The disk recorded the silence as Inga put her hand on Lit- man's arm to stop him. He looked up at her, and Frankie saw him see something in his sister's expression—his mother, maybe, his aunt?—that was enough to shut the light off on his smile. Frankie turned the recorder off, frowning. The thing was heavy and in the way. How was she to reach them with it sitting there like a small animal on her lap?

The mother slipped a piece of bread from her bag and handed it to her little boy. Everyone watched him eat. The woman in the corner stared fixedly out of the window. Frankie wondered whether she was deaf.

The young man in the sweater pulled a string from his pocket and wove the string between his fingers in a game of cat's cradle and held it up to the brother, who shook his head stiffly, clearly too old for such childishness. The young man laughed at him and Frankie saw a row of broken teeth between his lips. When he turned to her, holding his two hands woven together by the child's game, she smiled back at him and slipped her thumbs and forefingers under his, drawing the string onto her own hand.

"And you, Fräulein, where are you heading?" The man spoke in heavily accented but precise English, repeating Frankie's phrase.

"With all of you," Frankie answered as he looped his fingers in the string and pulled. He frowned.

"I'm riding this train to tell America who is on it."

He studied her. "Why?"

"So people know."

"What are you?"

"A reporter."

"So?" He let his fingers drop and the string went slack upon them. "And what is that box?"

"It records you, your voices." She sat back. "Sound."

"And what does America think?"

"America doesn't know what to think."

He nodded and crossed his arms, then his light, appraising gaze flicked off. The stubble on his chin was blond and sparse. "Shall I tell America what to think?"

"Shoot." She smiled at him.

He paused.

"Hold on." Frankie put her hand up. "Hold on." She pointed to the machine. He nodded. "Start," she said, switching the knob on the top, "slowly."

"I am Thomas Kleinmann—"

She looked up and saw he was holding out his hand to her and she reached across the spinning disk and shook it. "Frankie Bard."

He let go her hand and leaned back. "I come from Austria, in the mountains around Kitzbühel, where I live with my mother and father." He stopped. She nodded, go on. The disk whirled around.

"In the months after the Anschluss, after Austria fell to the Nazis and the Jewish laws were put into place there, my mother worried more and more about my brother, who was studying in Munich. Finally one day, she sent me to bring him back home."

Litman had slid his hand under Inga's beside him, quieting to listen to a story in words they did not understand.

"I travel all night on the train, arriving in the city early in the morning. I make my way to my brother's address, but my brother has left that same morning, according to the neighbor, to return home. We have crossed paths.

"I sit down at my brother's desk to write our mother and father and tell them what happened, but before I begin, there is a knock on the door. I shove the letter into my pocket and I go to answer. The police. They have come for Reinhart. Why? I ask. They do not answer. He is not here, I say. They take me instead. It does not matter to them"—Thomas shrugged—"which Jew they have."

The woman in the corner sucked in her breath. Frankie glanced up, realizing that the woman understood very well what was being said.

"I walk through the streets with a group of twenty others. We go to the police station, I am put into a room. Wait, they say. So, I am waiting, I pull out of my pocket the piece of stationery for my letter to Mother. It has on it the name of my brother's professor and the letterhead of the electrical engineering college. So, I write myself a letter of recommendation and take it to the policeman at the head of the room."

"Ah, says the guard, looking at it, go through there. I follow where he points and go into a tiny room where a large man, a friendly man, sits behind a pile of papers. This man looks at my letter, looks at me, and tears it in half. Go, he says, and points through another door. It is the door into the police yard. Out there, sixty or seventy men sit. No one looks at me. I walk all the way to the fence. I can see the river and the gardens behind houses.

"By this time it is afternoon, and the sun is very hot in the square. I walk along the fence and I stand in the little shade of the roof. For two hours I stand there and then there comes the instruction to go into the center of the square for new orders. Hsst, I hear at my shoulder. I turn around and see the guard I had spoken with earlier that morning, the guard to whom I had shown the letter. Hsst, the guard says and points me along the fence to a door. I look around. Is this is a trick? Is anyone watching? But there are just many men tired getting to their feet, and I go along the fence and out the door, a miracle. The guard is holding it open.

" '*Elektrotechnik?*' The guard grins. 'Professor Peter Schmidt?' I nod, dumbly, I don't understand. He points me to walk through the door and points to a second door, ten meters away, where another guard sits. I look at him, but the guard nods, go on, and pushes.

"I walk forward. I am not breathing. I reach the second guard. I can see the walk by the river beyond the police station and people returning from market. I stop and look at the guard. He doesn't look up. He reaches over and unlocks the gate.

"For twenty meters I walk straight ahead. Will I be shot, or shouted at, seen? Thirty meters. Now I am walking in the street. After forty meters, I know that I am free. I turn the corner at last. I am hurrying toward my brother's apartment, and I understand—it hits me, yes—I am out because the guard studied *Elektrotechnik* also."

He looked at Frankie and shook his head, his disbelief palpable in the dark.

"Then you are the lucky one here," the old woman in the corner broke in.

It was as if a shadow had spoken. "It is you," she repeated, in English. "There was God," she insisted. "Looking out for you, at every turn."

"People looked out"—he cleared his throat—"not God."

"The same."

He shook his head. "There is no God." He turned to Frankie, his voice urgent and low. "There is only us, Fräulein."

The train shuddered, slowing for another stop. Frankie turned the knob and the recording arm lifted off the disk. They had reached the German border at Kehl. On the other side lay Vichy France: Strasbourg, Lyon, Toulouse. And then on past France to Portugal, to the ships at Lisbon.

The lights of this station were blinding and numerous, and everyone was ordered off the train. Frankie stood.

"Except Americans."

Frankie looked up in surprise, but the German officer had passed down the compartment.

"Auf Wiedersehen." Litman waved to Frankie. She nodded, confused. Were they going to get back on this same train? What was happening? Litman and Inga were the first out of the compartment, followed by Werner Buchman, the tradesman who carried the young mother's bag, while she carried the sleeping Franz. Slowly, the old woman, whose name Frankie had never gotten, got to her feet, stiff after so many hours of sitting. She

turned around and looked at Thomas as if to take his image to heart. He bobbed his head at her, and reached up for his case on the rack as though he were following shortly after. The compartment door slid shut after the old woman, and Frankie stood to take the seat she had left by the window. It was slightly warm and Frankie reached and opened the window, letting the night air into the compartment.

"Now I must ask you to hide me," Thomas said, very low.

Frankie didn't move.

"I have the transit papers," he went on quickly, "but no exit visa."

She stared back.

"You understand?"

She nodded. Her heart was banging against her ribs. He looked at her briefly once more, and then he swung himself up onto the luggage rack and slid himself behind the suitcase. Frankie forced herself to look away from him and out the window at the people below, suddenly anonymous again, her companions from the compartment dispersed into the crowd. After a few minutes, she caught sight of the curly head of the mother and her little boy, and was comforted.

Frankie kept her eye on them, loosely following their progress in the dim light. It was too early to know whether to be afraid. The stop might be, even now, even after all that had happened, just routine. Some of the people had turned expectantly toward the station, facing it as though some kind of answer might come from it, some promise of order; but the mess of people on the platform below didn't move, and some simply sat down in place to wait. Above her on the luggage rack, Thomas lay still. Frankie closed her eyes and dozed a little and when she woke from time to time, she'd look down into the crowd to mark the progress of the woman and the little boy. After an hour or so, three black cars pulled up alongside the train and the border guards on the platform began shouting for people to get up and move down toward the end. Frankie saw the mother struggling up to her feet, then drop as though she had tripped or been pushed. When she rose again at the height of the crowd, she was looking frantically around, and Frankie saw that little Franz was gone. The crowd surged forward, shoving toward a gap at the end of the platform. Frankie scrambled to her feet and onto her seat, trying to see down into the crowd and catch sight of the child, but all she could see was the mother trying to stand against the push of the crowd. The man behind her shouted, *MOVE, we're moving!* and there were whistles, and two guards shouted at the mother and one grabbed her arm to come away. And then Frankie saw the boy—twenty impossible, unreachable feet from his mother.

"There!" Frankie cried out. "There he is!"

At the same time as Frankie shouted, his mother had caught the sound of his crying and started pushing against the human tide to get at him. People roared at her and shoved back and the boy, hearing her cries, cried back, *Mama! Mama!*

"There!" Frankie shouted again, frantic. The mother could not get at her child. "There he is!"

Mama, Franz was wailing. *Mama, Mama!*

"Shut up, Fräulein," Thomas hissed at her. "They're going to shoot. For God's sake, shut up!"

"There!" Frankie pounded against the window. And one of the German officers, disgusted by the commotion, turned around and shot.

The crowd went silent. Hands that had been waving dropped. Truly frightened people did not scream, Frankie saw—they went quiet, they went watchful. Had he shot into the crowd? Had someone been hit? It was too hard to tell. There were too many. Where was the mother? Frankie stood at the open window, her mouth still in the shape of her cry. And then the officer who was a few feet from her window looked up at where the sound of her banging had come from and slowly leveled his revolver on her. She stared back at him, both hands on the glass, unable to breathe. And then she was yanked down off the seat by Thomas and pulled away from the window onto the floor. Outside the train, the quiet continued and the two of them lay there, Frankie sobbing into her hands, too frightened to look up. She couldn't bear the quiet. What had she done? Her heart was pounding so fast, she thought she was going to be sick. Someone shouted. Frankie looked over at Thomas who was sitting up, his ear against the compartment wall. Perhaps the soldier hadn't seen Thomas, perhaps from the outside it had merely looked like she had fallen backward off her seat.

The floor beneath them shuddered and bucked, and very slowly the train began to move again with the two of them inside. Frankie caught Thomas's eye, but he shook his head. What had happened? The roof of the station slid past in the window above her head. The train was going to leave the boy and his mother behind. *Halt! Halt!* Shouting broke out along the platform, but Frankie couldn't tell if it came from the people or from one of the soldiers. The train kept going, moving along almost to the end of the station. Where it stopped.

Frankie's heart heaved and dropped and she looked at Thomas sitting across from her on the floor in the dark compartment. For a moment there wasn't a sound, and she thought they might start off again, but then a whistle blew nearby and the carriage door was thrown open. Someone came up the steps and along the corridor; the compartment door slid back. She looked up at an officer of the Gestapo. Behind him, another man waited.

The officer bowed to her and asked her to get up on her feet. Very politely, she and Thomas were asked to come down off the train. Polite, and their guns were not drawn. There was something wrong with the engine. There was a bus waiting. Could they come, please. Numbly, Frankie reached for her suitcase and the disk recorder and passed down the corridor, aware of the three men behind her. The train had evidently been halted in the field just past the station. She climbed down the steps of the train onto the grass by the side of the train tracks. There was, in fact, a bus waiting; inside it, Frankie made out the heads of three others. First, there was the issue of papers.

"Is something wrong?" She faced the Germans.

"No, no," the first officer answered mildly, "nothing." But Frankie saw him change his grip on the gun in his hand, and a sick dread rose up in her chest. She turned to Thomas, beside her. He had closed his eyes. "No," she whispered, and put her hand on Thomas's arm and felt how thin he was beneath the cloth.

"Step away, Fräulein." The officer was genial.

Frankie turned her back on the officer and spoke into Thomas's closed eyes. "Thomas"—her grip tightened on his arm—"Thomas?"

"Go on." He shook his head.

"Thomas," she whispered, "please. Let me—"

"Fräulein!"

Thomas opened his eyes and looked at her at the same time as Frankie felt herself roughly pushed aside and the officer took his shot. Thomas fell at Frankie's feet with a sigh.

Frankie blinked. The officer behind her stepped away. She

stared ahead at the empty spot in the air where Thomas had just stood. Slowly she turned around.

The officer's eyes slid from him to Frankie. She stared back at him.

"I could detain you."

Distantly, as if from another lifetime, from inside the station, the telephone rang.

Across the field it rang twice, three times, four. Someone answered it. The officer looked up and, with an expression of disgust, he waved Frankie toward the bus. Shaking, she bent to pick up her suitcase and the recorder, looking one last time at Thomas. Blood streamed from his ear and across his neck into the ground. She whimpered.

"Go."

She turned around, and she walked away from Thomas, from the boy and from his mother somewhere back there on the station platform. She walked ten feet down the tracks away from the police before she started weeping. She walked a few more feet, waiting to hear a shot, waiting to hear a shout, anything at all. She lifted her arm and wiped the tears off on her sleeve. Between the train behind her and the bus ahead on the country lane there was nothing but the sound of her own breathing and her feet clipping stones and then the cool metal of the rail that she grabbed as she climbed on.

from

The Solitude of
Prime Numbers

by

Paolo Giordano

**"Mesmerizing . . . An exquisite rendering of what
one might call feelings at the subatomic level."**
—*The New York Times*

*A prime number is a lonely thing. It can only be divided
by itself or by one; it never truly fits with another. Alice
and Mattia, both "primes," are misfits haunted by early
tragedies. When the two meet as teenagers, they recognize in
each other a kindred, damaged spirit. Years later, a chance
encounter reunites them and forces a lifetime of concealed
emotion to the surface. But can two prime numbers ever
find a way to be together? This brilliantly conceived and
elegantly written debut novel by the youngest winner ever of
the prestigious Premio Strega award has sold more than one
million copies in Italy.* The Solitude of Prime Numbers *is a
stunning meditation on loneliness, love, and what it means
to be human.*

Mattia deliberately made all his movements as silently as he could. He knew that the chaos of the world would only increase, that the background noise would grow until it covered every coherent signal, but he was convinced that by carefully measuring his every gesture he would be less guilty of that slow ruin.

He had learned to set down first his toe and then his heel, keeping his weight toward the outside of the sole to minimize the amount of surface area in contact with the ground. He had perfected this technique years before, when he would get up in the night and stealthily roam about the house, the skin of his hands having become so dry that the only way to know they were still his was to pass a knife over them. Over time that strange, circumspect gait had become his normal way of walking.

His parents would often find themselves suddenly face-to-face with him, like a hologram projected from the floor, a frown on his face and his mouth always tightly shut. Once his mother dropped a plate with fright. Mattia bent down to pick up the bits, but resisted the temptation of those sharp edges. His mother, embarrassed, thanked him, and when he left she sat on the floor and stayed there for a quarter of an hour, defeated.

Mattia turned the key in the front door. He had learned that by turning the handle toward himself and pressing his palm over the keyhole, he could eliminate almost entirely the metallic click of the lock. With the bandage on it was even easier.

He slipped into the hallway, put the keys back in again, and repeated the operation from inside, like a burglar in his own home.

His father was already home, earlier than usual. When he heard him raise his voice he froze, unsure whether to cross the sitting room and interrupt his parents' conversation or go out again and wait until he saw the living room light go out from the courtyard.

"I don't think it's right," his father concluded with a note of reproach in his voice.

"Right," Adele shot back. "You'd rather pretend nothing is wrong, act as if nothing strange were going on."

"And what's so strange?"

There was a pause. Mattia could picture his mother lowering her head and wrinkling up one corner of her mouth as if to say it's pointless trying to talk with you.

"What's so strange?" she repeated emphatically. "I don't . . ."

Mattia kept a step back from the ray of light that spilled from the sitting room into the hall. With his eyes he followed the line of shadow from the floor to the walls and then to the ceiling. He realized that it formed a trapezoid, only one more trick of perspective.

His mother often abandoned her sentences halfway through, as if she had forgotten what she was going to say as she was saying it. Those interruptions left bubbles of emptiness in her eyes and in the air and Mattia always imagined bursting them with a finger.

"What's strange is that he stuck a knife in his hand in front of all his classmates. What's strange is that we were convinced those days were over but we were wrong once again," his mother went on.

Mattia had no reaction when he realized that they were talking about him, just a mild sense of guilt at eavesdropping on a conversation he wasn't supposed to hear.

"That's not reason enough to go and talk to his teachers without him," his father said, but in a more moderate tone. "He's old enough to have the right to be there."

"For God's sake, Pietro," his mother exploded. She never called him by name. "That's not the point, don't you understand? Will you stop treating him as if he were—"

She froze. The silence stuck in the air like static electricity. A slight shock made Mattia's back contract.

"As if he were what?"

"Normal," his mother confessed. Her voice trembled slightly and Mattia wondered if she was crying. Then again, she cried often since that afternoon. Most of the time for no reason. Sometimes she cried because the meat she had cooked was stringy or because the plants on the balcony were full of parasites. Whatever the reason, her despair was always the same. As if, in any case, there were nothing to be done.

"His teachers say he has no friends. He only talks to the boy who sits next to him and he spends the whole day with him. Boys his age go out in the evening, try to hook up with girls—"

"You don't think he's . . ." his father interrupted. "Well, you know . . ."

Mattia tried to complete the sentence, but nothing came to mind.

"No, that's not what I think. Maybe I wish that's all it was," said his mother. "Sometimes I think that something of Michela ended up in him."

His father let out a deep, loud sigh.

"You promised not to talk about that anymore," he said, vaguely irritated.

Mattia thought of Michela, who had disappeared into thin air. But only for a fraction of a second. Then he let himself be distracted by the faint image of his parents, who, he discovered, were reflected in miniature on the smooth, curved surfaces of the umbrella stand. He started scratching his left elbow with his keys. He felt the joint twitching from one tooth to the next.

"Do you know what really makes me shiver?" said Adele. "All those high grades he gets. Always the highest. There's something frightening in those grades."

Mattia heard his mother sniff, once. She sniffed again, but now it sounded as if her nose were pressed up against something. He imagined his father taking her in his arms, in the middle of the living room.

"He's fifteen," said his father. "It's a cruel age."

His mother didn't reply and Mattia listened to those rhythmic sobs rising to a peak of intensity and then slowly ebbing, finally growing silent again.

At that point he walked into the living room. He closed his eyes slightly as he entered the beam of light. He stopped two steps away from his hugging parents, who looked at him in alarm, like two kids caught necking. Stamped on their faces was the question, how long had he been out there?

Mattia looked at a point midway between them. He said, simply, I do have friends, I'm going to a party on Saturday. Then he continued toward the hall and disappeared into his room.

I I

The tattoo artist had eyed suspiciously first Alice and then the woman with the too dark skin and the frightened expression whom the girl had introduced as her mother. He didn't believe it for a second, but it was none of his business. He was used to tricks of that kind, and he was used to capricious teenage girls. They were getting younger and younger: this one couldn't be as much as seventeen, he thought. But he certainly wasn't in a position to refuse a job for a question of principle. He'd shown the woman to a chair, and she'd sat down and hadn't said another word. She had gripped her purse tightly in her hands, as if ready to leave at any moment, and looked everywhere except in the direction of the needle.

The girl hadn't flinched. He had asked does it hurt, because that's something you have to ask, but she had said no, no through clenched teeth.

He had recommended that she keep the gauze on for at least three days and to clean the wound morning and evening for a week. He had given her a jar of Vaseline and stuffed the money in his pocket.

Back home in the bathroom, Alice took off the white tape that held the bandage on. Her tattoo had been in existence for only a few hours and she had already peeked at it a dozen times. Each time she looked, a bit of the excitement dispersed, like a pool of shimmering water that evaporates beneath the August sun. This time she thought only of how red her skin had turned, all the way around the design. She wondered if her skin would ever regain its natural color and for a moment her throat tightened with panic. Then she banished that stupid anxiety. She hated the fact that her every action always had to seem so irremediable, so definitive. In her mind she called it *the weight of consequences,* and she was sure that it was another awkward piece of her father that had wormed its way into her brain. How she longed for the uninhibitedness of kids her age, their vacuous sense of immortality. She yearned for all the lightness of her fifteen years, but in trying to grasp it she became aware of the fury with which the time at her disposal was slipping away. The weight of consequences was becoming more and more unbearable and her thoughts began whirling faster and faster, in ever smaller circles.

She had changed her mind at the last moment. That was what she had said to the young man who had already turned on the whizzing machine and was bringing the needle to her belly: I've changed my mind. Unsurprised, he had asked her don't you want to do it anymore? Alice had said yes I want to. But I don't want a rose. I want a violet.

The tattooist had looked at her, puzzled. Then he had confessed that he didn't exactly know what a violet looked like. It's kind of like a daisy, Alice had explained, only with three petals at the top and two at the bottom. And it's violet in color. The tattooist had said okay and set to work.

Alice looked at the livid little flower that now framed her navel and wondered if Viola would understand that it was for her, for their friendship. She decided she wouldn't show it to her till Monday. She wanted to present it without any scabs, bright against her pale skin. She chided herself for not doing it earlier, so that it would have been ready for tonight. She imagined what it would be like to show it secretly to that boy she'd invited to the party. Two days before, Mattia had appeared in front of her and Viola, with that sunken air of his. Denis and I are coming to the party, he had said. Viola hadn't even had time to come up with an unpleasant remark before he was already at the far end of the hall, his back turned to them and head lowered.

She wasn't sure she wanted to kiss him, but it was all decided now and she would look like an idiot in front of Viola if she backed down.

She measured the precise point where the top of her underpants had to come to be able to see the tattoo but not the scar immediately below it. She slipped on a pair of jeans, a T-shirt, and a sweatshirt big enough to cover the lot—the tattoo, the scar, and the bumps of her hips—and then left the bathroom, to join Soledad in the kitchen and watch her make her special cinnamon dessert.

12

Denis took deep, long breaths, trying to fill his lungs with the smell of Pietro Balossino's car. A slightly sour smell of sweat, which seemed to emanate not so much from the people as from the fireproof seat covers, and from something damp that had been sitting there too long, perhaps hidden under the mats. Denis felt the mixture wrap around his face like a hot bandage.

He would happily have spent all night in that car, driving around the half-dark streets of the hill, watching the lights of the cars in the opposite lane strike his friend's face and then return it to the shadows, unharmed.

Mattia was sitting in the front, beside his father. To Denis, who had been secretly studying the absence of any expression on both their faces, it seemed that father and son had agreed not to utter a single word during the whole journey, and to ensure that their eyes didn't meet even by accident.

He noticed that they had the same way of holding objects, framing them with their fingers tensed, touching surfaces but not really resting on them, as if they feared deforming whatever they held in their hands. Mr. Balossino seemed to barely touch the steering wheel. Mattia's frightful hands traced the edges of the present that his mother had bought for Viola and which he now held on his knees.

"So you're in the same class as Mattia," Mr. Balossino forced himself to say, though without much conviction.

"Yeah," said Denis, in a shrill voice that seemed to have been trapped for too long in his throat. "We sit next to each other."

Mattia's father nodded seriously and then, his conscience assuaged, he returned to his thoughts. Mattia seemed not even to have noticed that scrap of conversation and didn't take his eyes off the window, through which he was trying to work out whether his perception that the dotted white line in the middle of the road was in fact a continuous line was due merely to his eye's slow response or to some more complicated mechanism.

Pietro Balossino braked a few feet away from the big gate of the Bai family's property and put on the hand brake as they were on a slight incline.

"She's pretty well off, your friend," he observed, leaning forward to see over the top of the gate.

Neither Denis nor Mattia admitted that they barely knew the girl's name.

"So I'll come back for you at midnight, okay?"

"Eleven," Mattia replied quickly. "Let's make it eleven."

"Eleven? But it's already nine o'clock. What are you going to do for only two hours?"

"Eleven," insisted Mattia.

Pietro Balossino shook his head and said okay.

Mattia got out of the car and Denis did likewise, reluctantly. He was worried that Mattia might make new friends at the party, fun, fashionable friends who, in the bat of an eye, would take him away forever. He was worried that he would never get into that car again.

He politely said good-bye to Mattia's father and, to seem like a grown-up, held out his hand. Pietro Balossino performed a clumsy acrobatic maneuver to shake it without unfastening his seat belt.

The boys stood stiffly at the gate and waited for the car to turn around before deciding to ring the bell.

Alice was crouching at one end of the white sofa. A glass of Sprite in her hand, from the corner of her eye she was peeking at Sara Turletti's voluminous thighs, crammed into a pair of dark tights.

Squashed onto the sofa they became even bigger, almost twice as broad. Alice thought about the space she occupied compared to her classmate. The idea of being able to become so thin as to be invisible gave her a pleasant pang in the stomach.

When Mattia and Denis came into the room, she suddenly stiffened her back and looked around desperately for Viola. She noticed that Mattia wasn't wearing a bandage anymore and tried to see if he had a scar on his wrist. She instinctively ran her index finger along the trace of her own scar. She knew how to find it even under her clothes; it was like an earthworm lying against her skin.

The boys looked around like hunted prey, but in truth not one of the thirty or so kids scattered around the room paid them the least attention. No one except Alice.

Denis followed Mattia's movements, going where he went and looking where he looked. Mattia walked over to Viola, who was busy telling one of her made-up stories to a group of girls. He didn't even ask himself whether he'd ever seen those girls at school. He stood behind the birthday girl, holding the present stiffly to his chest. Viola turned around when she noticed that her friends had taken their eyes off her irresistible mouth and were looking instead over her shoulder.

"Ah, you're here," she said rudely.

"Here," said Mattia, placing the present in her arms. Then he added a mumbled happy birthday.

He was about to go when Viola shouted in an overexcited voice, "Alice, Alice, come quickly. Your friend's here."

Denis swallowed the lump in his throat. One of Viola's little friends cackled into another girl's ear.

Alice got up from the sofa. In the four paces that separated her from the group she tried to mask her syncopated gait, but she was sure that that was what they were all looking at.

She greeted Denis with a quick smile and then Mattia, bowing her head and saying hi in a faint voice. Mattia said hi back and his eyebrows jerked, making him appear even more spastic in Viola's eyes.

There followed an uncomfortably long silence that only she was able to break.

"I've discovered where my sister keeps the pills," she said, beaming. "Do you want some?"

She aimed her question at Mattia, certain that he wouldn't have the slightest idea what she was talking about. She was right.

"Girls, come with me, let's go get them," she said. "You too, Alice."

She took Alice by an arm and the five girls jostled one another as they disappeared down the hall.

Denis was alone with Mattia again and his heartbeat resumed its regular frequency. They both walked over to the drinks table.

"There's whiskey," Denis observed, slightly shocked. "And vodka too."

Mattia didn't reply. He took a plastic cup from the stack and filled it to the brim with Coca-Cola, trying to get as close as possible to that limit where the surface tension of the liquid prevents it from spilling over. Then he set it down on the table. Denis poured himself some whiskey, looking cautiously around and hoping secretly to impress Mattia, who didn't even notice.

Two rooms away, the girls had sat Alice down on Viola's sister's bed to instruct her about what to do.

"No blow jobs. Not even if he asks you, understand?" advised Giada Savarino. "The first time the max you can do is a hand job."

Alice laughed nervously and couldn't work out whether Giada was being serious.

"Now, you go back in there and start talking to him," explained Viola, who had a plan in mind and a very clear one. "Then you come up with an excuse to take him to my room, okay?"

"And what excuse am I supposed to come up with?"

"How do I know? Anything. Tell him you're fed up with the music and you want some peace and quiet."

"What about his friend? He's always glued to him," Alice said.

"We'll take care of him," said Viola with her most ruthless smile.

She climbed onto her sister's bed, trampling the light green cover with her shoes. Alice thought of her father, who wouldn't even let her walk on the carpet with her shoes on. For a second she wondered what he would have said if he had seen her there, but then she swallowed back the thought.

Viola opened a drawer in the cupboard above the bed. She rummaged around, not tall enough to see inside, and took out a little box covered with red fabric, adorned with gilded Chinese characters.

"Take this," she said. She held her hand out toward Alice. In the middle of her palm was a bright blue pill, square and with rounded corners. Carved in the center was a butterfly. For a second Alice saw the filthy fruit gumdrop she had accepted from that very same hand and felt it trapped in her throat again.

"What is it?" she asked.

"Take it. You'll have more fun."

Viola winked. Alice thought for a moment. They were all looking at her. She thought this must be another test. She took the pill from Viola's hand and placed it on her tongue.

"You're ready," Viola said with satisfaction. "Let's go."

The girls left the room single file, all looking down and with wicked smiles on their faces. Federica pleaded with Viola, please, let me have one too. And Viola brusquely told her wait your turn.

Alice was the last to leave. When all their backs were turned, she brought a hand to her mouth and spat out the pill. She put it in her pocket and turned out the light.

13

Like four beasts of prey, Viola, Giada, Federica, and Giulia surrounded Denis.

"Will you come with us?" Viola asked.

"Why?"

"We'll explain why later," Viola cackled.

Denis froze. He sought Mattia's help, but Mattia was still absorbed in the quivering Coca-Cola. The loud music that filled the room made the surface jerk with each beat of the bass drum. Mattia waited with strange trepidation for the moment when it would spill over the rim.

"I'd rather stay here," said Denis.

"God, how boring you are," Viola said, losing her patience. "You're coming with us and that's that."

She pulled him by the arm. Denis resisted feebly. Then Giada started pulling as well and he gave in. As they were pushing him into the kitchen, he looked once more at his friend, who was still motionless.

Mattia became aware of Alice's presence when she rested a hand on the table: the tension broke and a thin layer of liquid spilled over the rim and settled around the base in a dark ring.

He instinctively looked up and met her gaze.

"How's it going?" she asked.

Mattia nodded. "Fine," he said.

"Do you like the party?"

"Mmm."

"Music this loud gives me a headache."

Alice waited for Mattia to say something. She looked at him and it seemed to her that he wasn't breathing. His eyes were meek and pain-stricken. Like the first time, she suddenly wanted to draw those eyes toward her, to take Mattia's head in her hands and tell him everything would be okay.

"Will you come into the other room with me?" she ventured.

Mattia looked at the floor, as if he had been waiting for those very words.

"Okay," he said.

Alice headed down the hall and he followed a short distance behind. Mattia, as always, kept his head down and looked in front of him. He noticed that Alice's right leg bent gracefully at the knee, like every other leg in the world, and her foot brushed the floor without a sound. Her left leg, on the other hand, remained stiff. To push it forward she had to make it do a little arc outward. For a fraction of a second her pelvis was unbalanced, as if she were about to topple sideways. At last her left foot touched the ground as well, heavily, like a crutch.

Mattia concentrated on that gyroscopic rhythm, and without realizing it he synchronized his steps with hers.

When they got to Viola's room, Alice sidled up next to him and, with a daring that startled even her, closed the door. They were standing, he on the rug and she just off it.

Why doesn't he say anything? Alice wondered.

For a moment she wanted to drop the whole thing, to open the door again and leave, to breathe normally.

But what would I tell Viola? she thought.

"It's better in here, isn't it?" she said.

"Yeah," Mattia agreed, nodding. His arms dangled at his sides like a ventriloquist's dummy. With his right index finger he was folding a short, hard bit of skin that stuck out from beside his thumbnail. It was almost like piercing himself with a needle and the sting distracted him for a moment from the charged air in the room.

Alice sat on Viola's bed, balancing on the edge. The mattress didn't dip beneath her weight. She looked around, searching for something.

"Why don't you sit down here?" she asked Mattia at last.

He obeyed, sitting down carefully, about a foot away from her. The music in the living room sounded like the heavy, panting breath of the walls. Alice noticed Mattia's hands, clenched into fists.

"Is your hand better?" she asked.

"Nearly," he said.

"How did you do it?"

"I cut myself. In the biology lab. By accident."

"Can I see?"

Mattia tightened his fists still further. Then he slowly opened his left hand. A furrow, light in shade and perfectly straight, cut it diagonally. Around it, Alice made out scars that were shorter and paler, almost white. They filled the whole of his palm, intersecting like the branches of a leafless tree seen against the light.

"I've got one too, you know," she said.

Mattia clenched his fist again and trapped his hand between his legs, as if to hide it. Alice stood up, lifted her sweatshirt slightly, and unbuttoned her jeans. He was seized by panic. He turned his eyes to the floor, but still managed to see Alice's hands folding back the edge of her trousers, revealing a piece of white gauze framed by Scotch tape and, just below it, the top of a pair of pale gray underpants.

Alice lowered the elastic band a couple of inches and Mattia held his breath.

"Look," she said.

A long scar ran along her protruding pelvis bone. It was thick and in relief, and wider than Mattia's. The marks from the stitches, which intersected it perpendicularly and at regular intervals, made it look like the kind of scar children draw on their faces when they dress up as pirates.

Mattia couldn't think what to say. Alice buttoned up her jeans and tucked her undershirt inside them. Then she sat down again, a little closer to him.

The silence was almost unbearable for both of them, the empty space between their faces overflowing with expectation and embarrassment.

"Do you like your new school?" Alice asked, for the sake of saying something.

"Yes."

"They say you're a genius."

Mattia sucked in his cheeks and bit into them till he felt the metallic taste of blood filling his mouth.

"Do you really like studying?"

Mattia nodded.

"Why?"

"It's the only thing I know how to do," he said shortly. He wanted to tell her that he liked studying because you can do it alone, because all the things you study are already dead, cold, and chewed over. He wanted to tell her that the pages of the schoolbooks were all the same temperature, that they left you time to choose, that they never hurt you and you couldn't hurt them either. But he said nothing.

"And do you like me?" Alice went for it. Her voice came out rather shrilly and her face exploded with heat.

"I don't know," Mattia answered hastily, looking at the floor.

"Why?"

"I don't know," he insisted. "I haven't thought about it."

"You don't need to think about it."

"If I don't think, I can't understand anything."

"I like you," said Alice. "A bit. I think."

He nodded. He played at contracting and relaxing his retina, to make the geometric design of the carpet go in and out of focus.

"Do you want to kiss me?" Alice asked. She wasn't ashamed, but as she said it her empty stomach curled with terror that he might say no.

Mattia didn't move for a few seconds. Then he shook his head, slowly, still staring at the swirls in the carpet.

With a nervous impulse, Alice brought her hands to her hips and measured the circumference of her waist.

"It doesn't matter," she said quickly, in a different voice. "Please don't tell anyone," she added.

You're an idiot, she thought. Worse than a girl in kindergarten.

She stood up. Suddenly Viola's room seemed like a strange, hostile place. She felt herself becoming intoxicated by all the colors on the walls, the desk covered with makeup, the toe shoes hanging from the closet door, like a pair of severed feet, the big photo of Viola at the beach, lying on the sand looking beautiful, the cassettes stacked haphazardly beside the stereo, and the clothes piled up on the armchair.

"Let's go back," she said.

Mattia got up from the bed. He looked at her for a moment, apologetically, it seemed to her. She opened the door, letting the music flood the room. She walked partway down the hall alone. Then she thought of Viola's face. She turned around, took Mattia's stiff hand without asking his permission, and together they walked into the noisy living room.

14

The girls had trapped Denis in the corner, near the fridge, so as to have a little fun. They had arranged themselves in front of him, forming a barrier of excited eyes and flowing hair, through which he could no longer see Mattia in the other room.

"Truth or dare?" Viola asked him.

Denis shook his head timidly, to say that he didn't feel like playing this game. Viola rolled her eyes and then opened the fridge, forcing Denis to lean to the side to make room for the door. She pulled out a bottle of peach vodka and took a gulp, without bothering to find a glass. Then she offered him some, with a complicit smile.

He already felt dizzy and a little nauseated. The whiskey had left a bitter aftertaste suspended between his nose and his mouth, but there was something in Viola's behavior that prevented him from objecting. He took the bottle and took a sip. Then he passed it to Giada Savarino, who grabbed it greedily and started to pour it down her throat as if it were orangeade.

"So. Truth or dare?" repeated Viola. "Otherwise we'll choose."

"I don't like this game," Denis objected unconvincingly.

"Mmm, you and your friend really are a drag," she said. "Then I'll choose. Truth. Let's see."

She rested her index finger on her chin and with her eyes traced an imaginary circle on the ceiling, pretending to be deep in thought.

"I know!" she exclaimed. "You have to tell us which one of us you like best."

Denis shrugged, intimidated.

"Dunno," he said.

"What do you mean, dunno? You must like at least one of us, right?"

Denis thought he didn't like any of them, that he just wanted them to get out of his way and let him get back to Mattia. That he had only one more hour to be with him and watch him exist, even at night, when usually the only thing he could do was imagine him in his bedroom, sleeping under a sheet the color of which he didn't know.

If I choose one of them, they'll leave me alone, he thought.

"Her." He pointed to Giulia Mirandi, because she seemed the most harmless.

Giulia brought a hand to her mouth as if she'd just been elected prom queen. Viola turned up one corner of her mouth. The other two exploded into coarse laughter.

"Good," said Viola. "So now the dare."

"No, that's enough," protested Denis.

"You really are a bore. Here you are, surrounded by four girls, and you don't even want to play a bit. Certainly this doesn't happen to you every day."

"But now it's someone else's turn."

"And I say it's still your turn. You have to do the dare. What do you say, girls?"

The others nodded greedily. The bottle was once more in the hands of Giada, who at regular intervals threw back her head and took a swig, as if she wanted to finish it before the others noticed.

"See?" said Viola.

Denis snorted.

"What do I have to do?" he asked with resignation.

"Well, since I'm a generous hostess, I'm going to give you a nice dare," Viola said mysteriously. The other three hung on her words, eager to discover the new torture. "You have to kiss Giulia."

Giulia blushed. Denis felt a pang in his ribs.

"Are you crazy?" Giulia asked, shocked, perhaps pretending.

Viola gave a capricious shrug. Denis shook his head no, two, three times in a row.

"You were the one who said you liked her," she said.

"What if I don't do it?"

Suddenly dead serious, Viola looked him straight in the eyes.

"If you don't do it you'll have to choose truth again," she said. "You could tell us about your little friend, for example."

In her keen, bright stare Denis recognized all the things he had always thought were invisible. His neck stiffened.

His arms at his sides, he leaned his face toward Giulia Mirandi, narrowed his eyes, and kissed her. Then he tried to draw back, but Giulia held his head, her hand on the back of his neck. She forced her tongue through his pursed lips.

In his mouth Denis tasted saliva that wasn't his own and felt sick. In the middle of this, his first kiss, he opened his eyes just in time to see Mattia coming into the kitchen, hand in hand with the crippled girl.